STAFFORDSHIRE
FOLK
TALES

THE JOURNEY MAN

The History Press

First published 2012

The History Press
The Mill, Brimscombe Port
Stroud, Gloucestershire, GL5 2QG
www.thehistorypress.co.uk

British Library Cataloguing in Publication Data.
A catalogue record for this book is available from the British Library.

ISBN 978 0 7524 6564 7

Typesetting and origination by The History Press
Printed in Great Britain

CONTENTS

ACKNOWLEDGEMENTS

In the compilation of this book, I have drawn on many sources and would like to thank all those who have told me stories, pointed me in the right direction and shown me some of the key sites around the county. I would particularly like to thank David Pott of the Two Saints Way, who took time out to lead me on the path of Wulfad and Rufin. I would also particularly like to acknowledge the work of three researchers who have gone before me: Jon Raven, Doug Pickford and Fred Leigh. These three have been like the Three Kings of Lichfield to me. In my own note taking, I reduced their work by cutting it into bits and pieces, providing me with some strong foundations, on which I have built to produce this book. So, I say thank you to all those who have gone before me, for recording much of this diverse and fascinating county of Staffordshire.

INTRODUCTION

Staffordshire is a county known for its potteries and its bull terrier. Others may know of its breweries and some may even be aware of how its southerly tip forms part of the Black Country. However, for most people it is a county you travel through to get to somewhere else. Those travelling north from London or Birmingham may have noted signs for Stafford or Stoke off the M6, and those travelling south to Wales may have had to pass through, their routes crossing one another like the Staffordshire Knot. However, this county is one with an amazing and intriguing folklore. It has its own tales of some of the nation's favourite mythic heroes. It is the county that produced some great thinkers of its own, such as Erasmus Darwin and Dr Samuel Johnson. And Lichfield was the home of the great actor David Garrick. But there are also some unique traditions, such as the horn dance of Abbots Bromley. The antlers used in this ritual have been proven to be around 1,000 years old, which suggests that the dance has been performed every year since the time of Ethelfleda. The people have their own array of sprites and things that go bump in the night, including Rawhead-and-Bloody-Bones and the Kidsgrove Boggart.

In fact, this county has an intriguingly intimate relationship with all of its bogeymen. I find this fascinating when considering the deeply religious, but often dissenting, nature of the county. Staffordshire has more than its fair share of saints, but in years it hosted Lollards and later birthed Primitive Methodism. Such evangelical traditions seem to have revelled in the folklore of the place, even if it was only to cast out the so-called demons.

Pilgrimages have passed through Staffordshire, and recent years have seen the reintroduction of the Two Saints Way, which ends at Lichfield. There are also the five rivers that pass through: the Dove, Sow, Trent, Tame and Anker. All have brought influences into the region. Not to mention the canals and all the tales of the boatmen. As well as being a greatly agricultural county, there has been a wide array of industries. Best known will be the potteries, but I could also mention the beer, bricks, irons, boots, shoes, textiles, chemicals and coal. As history and society progressed, these stories were told and retold, passed on from rural folk to industrialised society. And with every retelling, each generation made these tales their own. So the stories have rolled on through Staffordshire, but unlike that stone which gathers no moss, they have picked up something along the way, becoming tales that have very much a Staffordshire flavour, whether told in the potteries or told in the Black Country. With all this material then, I have had the challenge of deciding what to leave out of this collection, rather than struggling to find enough to fill it. I live in Cheshire, but I regularly work in this county, storytelling in many of its schools. It has therefore been an honour to receive the opportunity to put this collection of folk tales together. In doing so, I soon became aware that Staffordshire has a number of distinct regions. To the north, there are the Moorlands which have their own folklore.

Stoke and the other pottery centres have developed stories unique to their growth as industrial towns; while the Black Country is almost like a county in its own right. Put this together with the wonderful tales of Mercia's saints, who did so much in the area, and its own collection of spirits and bogeymen, and you will begin to see what I mean about the complexity of the region. I therefore decided to arrange this book into five sections, so reflecting the distinctions of the stories and folklore. They are as follows:

Bogeymen, Bugs and Black Dogs
Tales of the Moorlands
Tales from Mercian Staffordshire
Tales from the Middle
Tales of the Black Country

With many of these tales I have tried to maintain the flavour of Staffordshire folk culture. One element is the importance in the naming of towns and villages, many of which have strong connections with the stories of their origins – real or imagined. Another is the use of rhymes to capture events or tales. I have never found so many, and although this is a book of folk tales rather than folk songs, I have felt I could not effectively produce a book of Staffordshire tales without including a few rhymes. I was even inspired to write my own. The tale of the 'Three Kings of Lichfield' almost begged to be written in verse, and so I make my offering.

I owe much to the work of those three distinct authors mentioned in my acknowledgements. For folklore I have drawn on the iconic volume *The Folklore of Staffordshire* by Jon Raven, who also focuses much on the Black Country.

Doug Pickford has done much work in identifying many of the mystical locations, especially those on the Moorlands, collecting various anecdotes of people's intriguing experiences and making some interesting connections. And then there is the book *North Staffordshire: Myths and Legends*, in which Fred Leigh has embellished many of the fragmentary tales to create some enthralling short stories. My method is quite similar to Leigh's, in that I enjoy playing about with bits and pieces of stories, filling in the gaps, and bringing in other elements from the regional folklore and history. In doing so, my hope is that these tales continue to appeal to today's audience. Of course, I also hope that my humorous approach to the lives of many of Staffordshire's saints does not cause offence. I prefer to think of it as a gentle ribbing with some older siblings, rather than ridicule. Whether I use humour, fear, or lots of imagination, my aim has been to help you to connect with the spirit of Staffordshire. It is a county with so many fantastic stories, which often, like the Staffordshire Hoard, remain hidden to those who bustle on with their daily lives, speeding along the roads back and forth through the county. The fact that you are reading this introduction suggests that you are taking time out to sit down and enjoy some folk tales. So, do just that. Flip through the book and read whatever catches your eye. Or focus on one section at a time, learning its tales so that you can then visit those sites it speaks of. However you choose to read this book, my desire is that it opens your eyes to that beauty and wonder hidden just below the surface of Staffordshire.

The Journey Man, 2012

1

BOGEYMEN, BUGS AND BLACK DOGS

So let us begin by getting to know a few people. Some say that the people you know least are your neighbours, those who live shoulder to shoulder with you. However, the folk of Staffordshire may have had a host of unusual neighbours sharing their space. Although few may see them, they have a lot to say about them and have names for them all. Many are fearsome, or at least menacing, but despite this there is a certain amount of affection shown for the inhuman brood rubbing shoulders with the human residents of the county. There are names such as Lob-lie-by-the-fire and Will-o'-the-wisp, and a number of these bogeymen even have their own rhymes. The word 'bogeyman' is even shortened about the county, especially as you draw nearer the Black Country, to the less worrying 'bug'. These 'bugs' have fulfilled many purposes, from keeping children in check to warning miners and bargemen of imminent disasters, while others are a reminder of losses of life in the past. Of course, the infamous Spring Heel Jack is supposed to have made a number of appearances, but I have put his stories in with those of the Black Country. Here then are a number of bugs to get you started.

KIT CREWBUCKET

As the evening mist begins to rise on the canals, an eerie presence can be felt at the twin tunnels of Harecastle. As the temperature drops, a gentle but incessant outpouring of white cloudiness tumbles out of the entrances of those channels named Brindley and Telford, making the stories of Kit Crewbucket easily believed. If you take a barge into that darkness, you will soon come to the location of Gilbert's Hole, where the body of a woman was dumped after being murdered by three cruel boatmen. It is said that they hacked off her head with a piece of slate and it is here, in the middle of the tunnel, that some have seen her. Kit Crewbucket is what many call her, but she is perhaps more properly known as the Kidsgrove Boggart. Boggart is a fairly common word in the folklore of the West Midlands and the north-west of England. It describes a malevolent spirit, often associated with water. These female phantoms are said to have the ability to change shape. However, in the lore of these regions, the boggarts seem to remain in one form. Whether they are trapped in this shape or whether it is their favourite, I am not sure, but I don't plan on asking one. The further south you go in Staffordshire, the more likely you are to hear the word bug rather than boggart. This seems to me another indication of the familiarity of the residents with their spooks. As for the Kidsgrove Boggart, there are many stories to say who she was and how she came to be the way she is.

Unlike other boggarts, Kit Crewbucket was once human and her current form is in fact her ghost. The stories generally tell of a young woman who was travelling down the canal, but was the only female amongst a rough and cruel band of men. It was close to Kidsgrove that, after some miles of leers and threats, the men overcame the girl, attempted to have their wicked way with her and then killed her. Then, having dumped the decapitated body in the Harecastle tunnels, they continued on their journey. From that time on, people reported seeing a headless woman moving through the mist at the tunnel entrance. Others spoke of hearing screams echoing out of the tunnel. No one has been harmed by Kit Crewbucket, but her appearance and screams were understood to be warnings. Whenever there was a collision or disaster on that stretch of the canal, the Kidsgrove Boggart was seen beforehand. And so, as unnerving as it might have been to see a headless woman in the mist or hear blood-curdling screams echoing from the darkness of the tunnel, the bargemen did not avoid the tunnel out of fear of the bug, but more in obedience to her warnings.

So if she doesn't appear when you approach the Harecastle tunnels and all seems quiet, then you know that your journey on the water will be trouble free. However, if she does make her presence known, then go on your way with care.

RAWHEAD-AND-BLOODY-BONES

Rawhead-and-Bloody-Bones
Steals naughty children from their homes,
Takes them to his dirty den
And they are never seen again.

This bogeyman seems to be one of the more memorable and feared of the brood, and there may be some link here with Cheshire. On the Sandstone Ridge, one of the highest hills is named Rawhead, under which there is a large cave called the Queen's Parlour. It is said that the Bloody Bones Gang used to reside here. Many of the residents feared this band of grave-robbing, house-breaking individuals. Indeed, one girl named Isabella Bishop, from Tettenhall, wrote in her diary of how she had an accidental meeting with the gang and how they had tried to buy her silence. I have therefore often wondered if the Staffordshire rhyme and the Cheshire diary could be related. It could be argued that tales of the Bloody Bones Gang of Rawhead trickled down to Staffordshire, and the ideas of these shadowy figures were reformed into the bogeymen which were then used to frighten children into obedience. Some folk talk about him capturing children and throwing them into a black sack, presumably to take them to those caves in Cheshire – his dirty den. However, the rhyme seems to predate the Tettenhall diary entry by at least 100 years. Some have suggested that Miss Bishop's story was a fabrication – having heard the rhyme, she tied it to the neighbouring hill of Rawhead. Either way, the story of Rawhead-and-Bloody-Bones has taken on a life of its own. Some children believed that the bogeyman lived at the bottom of the pit shafts and they would challenge each other to shout the creature's name down the shaft. I doubt if any stayed to find out if there was an answer. On stormy nights, parents told their little ones that the howling wind was Rawhead-and-Bloody-Bones moaning as he looked for naughty children. Others were warned that he lived in the dark shadows of the cupboard under the stairs. This was presumably to keep children away from whatever their parents kept there, or to act as a warning that if they misbehaved they would be joining him. Stories of this creature have crossed the Atlantic too and are found in American folklore, as well as published short stories and novels. There is certainly something about the idea of Mr Bloody-Bones which inspires the darker side of the imagination.

DUMB BAW

Another bogeyman used for similar purposes, but based on a real person, is Dumb Baw. He was the son of a couple of colliers, Mr and Mrs Ball, and he was born without hearing and unable to speak. His parents didn't have the wherewithal to help him, or any idea how to care for him, and so young Ball would wander about the potteries of Staffordshire, sleeping wherever he pleased and taking whatever he could to eat. It was not long until this unfortunate became known to all as Dumb Baw. But despite the implications of his name, Ball was quick-witted and found ways of making money out of his situation. In many ways, he surprised folk as much as Dumb Dyott would have done – Dyott was the deaf and dumb marksman who shot an enemy down in the street whilst situated in one of the three towers of Lichfield Cathedral.

Ball knew that people dreaded him; they believed that he was possessed by the Devil in some way, and such dark forces were treated with interest, but also fear. After all, if he was connected with the Devil then maybe he could tell of secrets from the spiritual world. Ball knew he had no such powers, but if the belief was there then he was going to profit from it. He would tell fortunes to those who asked and paid. Taking a piece of chalk, he would mark out strange signs and figures which people believed to be magic. For the right payment he would use these to work out how many children a woman might have, or whether a girl was going to get married or not and when. With his chalk, he would write a number, and the people went away believing his predictions. He would even push his customers for a little more cash by suddenly looking panicked and drawing a coffin. Believing a death to be imminent, the panicking client would pay more money. Ball would then suddenly rub out the image and replace it with something more life-affirming, such as the sketch of a baby. Sadly, very few would befriend Ball, and children were unnerved by the gurgling and screeching sounds he was often heard to make. And so parents looking for a way to keep their children quiet would say: 'Hush now, I think I hear Dumb Baw coming!' Such a warning was still working over fifty years after Ball's own death!

WHITE RABBITS

In neighbouring Cheshire, a rather famous author not only popularised the idea of the Cheshire Cat, but also introduced the likeable but pathetic White Rabbit. White rabbits have been a symbol of good luck in English folklore for many years, but the charming image of a white rabbit dashing back and forth with the words 'Oh dear! Oh dear! I shall be too late!' may have darker origins.

The family of Clough Hall at Kidsgrove feared seeing a white rabbit cross their drive, as it was a portent of a death in the family. This association with death may come from the disturbing story of two boys from Burslem.

One day, two lads were whiling away the time in Etruria Grove. They were John Holdcroft and Charles Shaw and, as young men often do, they had a disagreement, which led to a fight. However, the tussle got out of hand, with John's anger towards the smaller Charles growing. Then, perhaps not knowing his own strength, the larger boy caught the other around

the neck and choked the life out of him. John was tried for murder but, in light of his young age, he escaped the noose to be transported instead. However, those who went to Etruria Grove after this tragic event would often say that they could hear the screams of a boy. But where they came from, they could not tell. Once the screams had died away, a mysterious white rabbit would come rushing out of the undergrowth, dashing across the path, before disappearing into the bushes on the other side. Sightings of the white rabbit were so prevalent that one local man decided to try to catch the creature. Although he saw it, his trapping attempts were not successful. He, in fact, had to call off the endeavour because he slipped and dislocated his shoulder. Many said that this was a sign that the white rabbit should be left alone and so, to this day, no one has caught the creature which dashes out of the leaves, resembling Lewis Carroll's creation.

White rabbits have also been associated with the magical. Witches have often been thought to have the ability to change shape, such as in the story of the 'Black Cat of Getliffe's Yard', and a white rabbit seems to have been a popular choice. I am not entirely sure why a witch, who has some intelligence about her, would turn into a white rabbit. Firstly, they are easy to spot and would raise suspicion immediately. Secondly, a predator is likely to spot a white rabbit before one that's brown or black. Maybe it was something to do with style. Either way, the practice seems to have died out. Perhaps too many witches ended up as food for foxes.

Another reference to the white rabbits is made when referring to so-called 'wise men' in Staffordshire. A number of men professed to have magical powers and hired themselves out to chant incantations or make spells for people's healing and protection.

This role seems to have been more commonly fulfilled by women throughout Great Britain, but here in Staffordshire, men were also well known to provide this service. Referred to as White Rabbits, they would be especially popular with miners, weaving spells to ensure that those who entered the mines would be protected.

It is curious then that white rabbits figure so greatly in the folklore of Staffordshire. There is certainly something unusual about seeing a white rabbit in the wild and so, maybe these stories are explanations that made sense at one time. However, I can guarantee that should you come across a white rabbit in the wild, you will never look at it in the same way again.

RED SOCKS

A girl was playing hide-and-seek whilst she was staying at Broughton Hall and went to hide in the Long Gallery. She waited for quite some time, thinking that her friends would come in soon. She especially wanted to impress the boy who lived there and had heard his footsteps run past the door to the gallery. She waited for a little longer but began to get bored, so she carefully looked out and almost gasped aloud. There, standing by the window, was a boy. Fortunately, however, he was looking out through the panes and not towards her. The girl then moved very quietly out from her hiding place and edged over to the door. As she did so, she noticed how the boy was dressed in some kind of costume, the most noticeable thing being his red socks. Then she slipped out of the door and downstairs.

Later that afternoon, when the game was over and all the children were boasting about their hiding places, the girl told the boy whom she had hoped to impress that she had managed to sneak past him without him even noticing. He looked confused and insisted he had not been in the Long Gallery all day. The girl said that she had seen him quite plainly, or at least someone who looked very much like him. The only difference was that he was dressed in some kind of costume. Again the boy denied this and said that the girl was making it up. That was until she mentioned that the boy she had seen was wearing long red socks. The boy gasped and everyone who was half-listening fell silent. He went on to tell the girl about the ghost which sometimes appeared in the Long Gallery. It was supposed to be the ghost of a boy who was killed in a raid that had taken place back in the Civil War. That boy was said to have stood at the window watching the enemy soldiers ride into the grounds of the hall. One soldier saw him standing there, took aim with his pistol and shot the child dead through the glass. He was wearing red hose, like many rich boys of those days, and any who saw his ghost always commented on this. He was therefore known in the family as Red Socks and that must have been whom the girl had seen as she came out of her hiding place.

BLACK DOGS

Black dogs appear all over the country. Some say that they are the Devil incarnate. And Staffordshire has, of course, its own share of sightings. Some who have studied these manifestations more closely suggest that they appear in places along the trail of Bonny Prince Charlie. The most memorable apparition of this sort is probably the Black Dog of Sedgley.

There was a family living there who dreaded the Black Dog; it had become a legend in their family history as it was known to appear every so often. The creature was larger in size than any ordinary dog, being more like a pony, and it had a pair of enormous red eyes, like two burning coals in the dark. The Black Dog would very occasionally appear, choosing to follow any family member who was travelling home in the evening. Fearsome as this may be, it was more what this unwelcome escort represented than its appearance that caused such intense anxiety. The presence of the Black Dog of Sedgley meant a death in the family, and often the demise of the very person it followed home.

Th'Olde Lad

I am intrigued as to how different regions across the country respond to the Devil. This long-time enemy of humanity has been treated with every possible reaction, from intense fear to a jokey humour, almost as if he is simply a misguided family member. As the industrialisation of Staffordshire increased, and religious fervour alongside it, the Devil began to be associated more and more with the smoke and grime of the increasing number of factories, as can be seen in William Blake's 'Satanic Mills'. There developed then a number of rhymes along these lines in the Black Country. I believe these were a way for the people to deal with the change in their landscape and the grittiness of their day-to-day lives. There are many tales of the Devil in Staffordshire, especially from the high days of Methodism, when Satan was not only blamed for much of people's irrational behaviour, but was also reported as being present in the houses and establishments of those whose activities clashed with some of the more dignified ideals of society. Despite this emphasis on his damaging influence, Staffordshire refers to the Father of Lies almost affectionately, as th'Olde Lad, and tells tales of his dealings with saints, witches and the odd landlord.

2

TALES OF THE MOORLANDS

Let us begin this collection of folk tales in that mystical landscape known as the Staffordshire Moorlands. For starters, it can be a bit of a challenge simply working out where you are exactly. It's very easy, out there on the moors, to wander in and out of Staffordshire. You can unknowingly cross the county boundary into Cheshire, and if you happen to stray just a little way to the north you'll very quickly find yourself in the Peak District, which is generally thought of as Derbyshire. However, that stretch of moorland on the Staffordshire side is truly a magical and inspirational place. This is particularly seen on the approach from Blackshaw Moor, where you are greeted by a dramatic panorama of intimidating rock formations. They rise up suddenly, looking like a row of ancient fortresses, resolutely standing as guardians to this landscape of legends. Continue on into this harsh, bleak world and you will be surrounded by what resembles a great array of crude stone statues. They have the appearance of markers from a time long gone, as if giants piled high these stones to indicate their boundaries. And when the sunlight breaks through the darkening clouds that hang over that range, its rays focus on this hill or that. Almost as if the sun is shining down on chosen sites, highlighting each of those mystical monuments in turn. Venture further into the moors and you will see how the land itself suddenly drops away here and there with surprising twists and turns, as if some subterranean activity has caused the earth to fall in on itself, sucked down into unexpected cavities, so creating folds and valleys between the deep shadows of those jagged hills. It is not surprising then that these Moorlands have inspired some unique stories. Some are quite chilling, others quite charming, but all of them are captivating. Their whispers draw you back to clamber up and challenge those rugged hills again, to unlock the mysteries hidden in millennia of enchantment. And you'll look twice at those unusual features, wondering how true those stories may be.

The stones here in Staffordshire have proved deeply fascinating for generations of residents and visitors to the moors. That part of the Moorlands known as the Roaches, for instance, takes its name from the old French for 'rocks' (*les rochers*). It's not only rocky piles collected and forgotten by the giants. There are stones which have clearly been sculpted by wind and rain, with soft twists and a gentle smoothness to them, naturally moulded into shapes which call to the imagination. The Moorlands have more than their fair share of stones, such as the Heart Stone, the Serpentine Stones and the Winking Man. And there is also the Bawstone, which is said to possess healing powers, whilst other stones bring enchantment. Some have simply mesmerised the people, who continue to summon up stories and bizarre explanations for their presence, but there are others which make themselves part of people's lives. One such pair would be the Bridestones, which probably supported the entrance to a burial mound at one time. Much of that has disappeared, but the two support stones remain with a scattering of fallen stones around them, lying about as if they were discarded. The Bridestones stand tall and proud amongst these others, and in doing so they resemble a couple on their wedding day. It is said that engaged couples would come up to the stones seeking some assurance from them, a blessing from ages past which would ensure that their vows lasted 'till death we do part'. I have even heard it suggested that couples who wanted to get married, but could not afford the Christian ceremony, would come and make promises to each other in front of the Bridestones, either having God as their witness or calling upon some other deity represented, so they believed, by the stones themselves.

It's easy to believe in such ancient spirits when wandering these Moorlands, as the landscape lends itself to tales of fairies, mermaids and headless horsemen – as well as those humans who have disengaged for too long from mainstream society. There is also a resilient band of creatures hidden up here in the Moorlands that came to these lands in more recent times. None have been sighted recently, but every so often stories are told of the odd wallaby hopping out of the undergrowth up around the Roaches. It seems that in the 1930s, a private zoo fell on hard times and the owners were unable to keep the animals. The simplest thing to do was to release them into the surrounding heathland. There was a small band, about five, of those marsupials known quite simply as the Wallabies of the Roaches. But sightings over the years suggest that there could be as many as fifty, despite the snowy winters experienced fairly regularly up there on the Moorlands. I have also heard of three yaks and an antelope that were released, but there seem to have been no sightings of those. You'd certainly know it if you were faced with a yak.

What follows then are a number of tales showing the inspiration taken from that vastly lonely landscape. Some originate from the Staffordshire Moorlands themselves, while others are stories told by outsiders. However, they all give an insight into how the people of Staffordshire have viewed this mysterious corner of their county, whilst providing us with quite a varied collection of stories.

THE FAIRY FOLK OF THE MOORLANDS

One attraction of the Staffordshire Moorlands may be the chance of seeing fairies. Tales of fairy folk seem to be hidden behind every boulder and hedgerow, especially about the Cloud, a distinctive hill with a name that suggests something of the ethereal. In fact, many would gaze towards the Cloud from Leek in the hope of catching the legendary double sunset, and such events only add to the magic of the place.

Those who lived about here were glad of the fairies existing alongside them, as there are none better to confound the plans of witches. The mischievous ways and the strong magic of fairies were known to undo the witches' weaving of spells, especially those set to harm their fellow humans. In fact, many people would talk about how useful the fairies could be in all areas of life, if you paid them the proper respect. They would retrieve lost items, putting them in a place where you could easily find them, often somewhere you had already looked earlier without success. They would also stop those pesky hedgehogs from sucking on cows' udders at night. But many humans also suffered from the trickery and revenge of the little people. This could be dispensed through minor annoyances, such as a knitting needle falling out of the wool or hair clips falling out. And if they felt like it, they could make the dog bark without reason through the whole night. But their mischief could become more serious, as in the sad, but not uncommon, story of a woman whose child was swapped for a changeling.

A young mother was working outside one hot summer's day with her baby in tow. She carefully put the child down and set up an umbrella to protect its delicate skin from the baking sun. She had only left the child for a little while, but when she returned she was sure that the baby she found under the umbrella was not the one she had left there. She kept the child – she had little choice – but it showed itself to be lethargic, with little willingness to engage in the mother's playful games. It didn't grow very much and never learnt to talk. The day she had left it under the umbrella, the fairy folk had exchanged it for one of their own, the mother was sure. This is known as a changeling. However, despite this, the mother always showed love to the child, bringing it up as her own, because what could she do now, but care for it? It was whilst she was cleaning out a cupboard that this mother dis-covered something which proved to her that the fairies were happy with the kindness she had shown to the changeling. At the back of the cupboard, she found something she had never noticed before – a bundle of cloth. She pulled it out and hurriedly unravelled it to find that it contained a handful of coins. Enough to pay for everything the child would need for one year.

The following year the same happened. And the next year, the same again. So for three years the mother and child had everything they could possibly need. Yet, despite this, the child always looked sickly and its condition only worsened, until, at the age of three, the child died. And the mother never found any bundles of money again. Proof once more that this was a fairy child, and that the mother had done all that was required of her.

It was because of stories like this that Staffordshire mothers were keen to have their children christened as soon as possible. It was believed that the fairies could not take a child if they had been baptised. So, Staffordshire became known for christenings taking place two or three days after a child was born, with mothers being exceptionally vigilant during this short but vulnerable period.

The mother mentioned earlier did not actually see the fairies, but there are those who say they have. Older folk who live in and around Mixon talk about a good fairy who lived in the area called Old Nancy. Others say they have found tiny little

pipes in the fields about there, left behind by the fairies after one of their evening dances. There was a man at Leek who talked about the day he actually saw fairies dancing. Their favourite places for such activities are low, boggy meadows. The story goes that this elderly gentleman was taking a snooze after a long day working in the garden. It was just as the sun was going down. I wouldn't be surprised to find that it was a double sunset, but, either way, he was awoken from his forty winks by some high-pitched notes. He was sure it was music, like a tiny pipe or two being played. The old man looked about and saw at the end of the garden, where it dipped down, a few bright flashes of colour. Slowly sitting up, he could not believe that he was actually watching a circle of fairies dancing. A few of them were playing their pipes as the others daintily danced about in a ring. The man was so taken by the charming nature of the scene that he sat right up and started to clap along. But his crashing hands made the fairies stop and they turned to stare at the smiling man. 'Oh, that was lovely!' he said. 'Well done, my little ones. You know I must say that the one in the blue dances the best.' But despite the compliment, the fairies vanished in a second. The old man never saw them again, but that was not for want of trying. He was always ready to take a snooze in the garden. After all, it had worked before.

The old man seems to have been lucky, as fairies do not like to be seen by humans, and those who spy on them can suffer from their anger. There is a tale of one who saw the fairies each day, but was not allowed to let other humans find out. This is a tale from the Black Country where the fairies are more resilient and less compliant. You'll find their stories a little later in the book.

LUD'S CHURCH

Not so far from the Roaches, hidden in the earth itself, there is an unusual and entrancing feature known as Lud's Church. It is a deep gorge naturally formed in the rocky hill and has the appearance of a small maze with a collection of channels winding off from the main fissure, with one or two being interconnected. If you explore this feature yourself, you could easily believe any of the explanations of how it came to be called Lud's Church. Although, the word 'church' is used a little generously here, in my opinion; I think 'temple' or 'shrine' might be better.

It is said that on one occasion when the Danes came through Mercia, they stumbled upon this collection of rocky trenches. It is, after all, found in the Dane Valley. The site seems to have been the perfect place for them to perform their religious practices. In readiness for their battles with the Saxons, the Vikings tortured and killed those they had captured from previous skirmishes here, sacrificing them to Thor. There are very similar tales told of Thor's Stone at Thurstaston in Cheshire, which makes me wonder if British storytellers in the past just had it in for Vikings. Maybe they wove tales about the Vikings' supposed gruesome goings-on to explain some otherwise charming natural features. In this negative vein then, some say that a man named Lud was the leader of those Vikings (the very same Lud who is buried at Ludlow in Shropshire). His name is given to this supposed site of worship in the Staffordshire Moorlands, Lud's Church.

It is claimed that a man called Lud was riding over the Roaches and was totally unaware of this gorge – it is quite hard to find if you don't know what you're looking for. His horse was, however, quickly aware of the change in the landscape and suddenly stopped. Lud went flying off the horse and fell through a stony gap. He crashed to the bottom dead and his body lay there undiscovered – the horse was unable to say where he had gone of course. Over the years, the moss in that place continued to grow and slowly claimed the body as its own. And so began a transformation as he was gradually incorporated into the stone itself, a petrified man whose name is now remembered by those who called the place Lud's Church. Some say you can see him there still, if you look at the overhanging rocks closely enough. But there are many faces in the rocky walls of those trenches and he could be any number of them. Maybe others have fallen in and so become one with the stone – that's why there are so many faces.

Or do those faces refer to the other stories told of Lud's Church? One particular tale tells of another band of worshippers who sought a place where they could meet without detection: the Lollards of Lud's Church. Another suggests that this is the very place where Sir Gawain met the Green Knight.

THE LOLLARDS OF LUD'S CHURCH

For up to 100 years an elevated guardian would oversee all visitors to Lud's Church. It was a ship's figurehead, carved as a woman, which sat up on a rocky ledge high up out of reach. Eventually a wind knocked the effigy down to the floor of the chasm, where it remained lying in the mud for some years until finally it disappeared. This figure was originally placed at Lud's Church in 1862. It was put there by Philip Brocklehurst of Swythamley in memory of a young woman named Alice de Lud-Auk. And for her story we need to go back a few more centuries.

As the Reformation began to sweep across Europe, those who followed the teaching of Bible translator John Wycliffe became known as Lollards. Of course, anyone dissenting from the Church's official teachings and translating the Bible into English was outlawed. Many had to go into hiding and, what with Staffordshire's strong tradition for dissenting, stories abounded of religious folk meeting in rocky outdoor places. So it was with the de Lud-Auk family.

Walter de Lud-Auk led his family and followers across the moors. They were searching for somewhere they could meet, somewhere hidden but a place that spoke of the holiness of God. Walter, amongst others, had with him his granddaughter, Alice. He had looked after the girl as if she was his own daughter. Her parents had both died when she was a child and she had grown into a tall and beautiful young woman. She had always responded well to teaching and had matured into someone known for being learned and resourceful. As the party searched for this wished-for place, tired and hungry, it was Alice who spotted a host of bilberry plants. Falling on them the party refreshed themselves, with that tiny but delicious fruit. Miniature explosions of crisp juiciness burst in the Dissenters' mouths as they thanked God for such provision.

'We are like the Children of Israel,' laughed Alice, encouraging her grandfather's followers. Her voice was clear and strong, ringing out over the rocks. 'As the Lord provided for them in wilderness, so he is proved faithful to us here in our own …'

And then she stopped, for she saw something just a little beyond the bilberries. It seemed to be a passage, hidden by clumps of plants. On her knees, Alice pushed her way through the crowd of leaves and saw below her the chambers of a hidden gorge. She called back to her grandfather and together they stepped down into that open-roofed tunnel.

'Alice, is this not the perfect place for us to meet?' said Walter, now looking up at the high sides of the trench. 'Why, we could worship here and none would be aware that we are nearby, even if they were to stop for bilberries themselves.'

That gathered host of Lollards entered the trench under Alice's guidance and now thanked the Lord that such a place had been provided.

This then is where these Christians met, but in secrecy. To keep this location to themselves they only referred to the spot as Lud's Church. It was a name chosen using part of their leader's surname, so only they knew what they were talking about if it should be mentioned in other company. Of course, they could not use the whole surname. That would be far too dangerous. Such meetings were illegal and could result in death sentences.

This band of the faithful then met at Lud's Church in the summer months of the year, when the road was less treacherous and the gorge was at its driest. Here they would read translations of the Bible in English and sing hymns together. Alice, with her clear and melodious voice, would bring lessons to the gathering, speaking out in that space to encourage the people in their faith.

It was soon noted by others, however, that the de Lud-Auk family were disappearing for days at a time and taking people with them. Word reached the authorities, and search parties were then sent out to the Dane Valley. They combed the moors for these Lollards, looking to catch them with their English Bibles and put an end to their heretical behaviour.

Eventually, an officer came across the entrance to Lud's Church. As he pushed through the bilberry plants, he heard the words of Alice exhorting the faithful from within the

chamber. Quickly he summoned his men and they lined up
to march along the rocky passage. But suddenly before them
appeared a great tall man whose broad shoulders blocked
their way. He was Henrich Montair, the Chief Forester, and
he was one of Walter de Lud-Auk's number. The officer was
surprised not only to see such a giant in his way, but that a
man of such standing should be associating with this ragtag
gang of heretics. Henrich seized his moment and with a great
hand shoved the officer heartily. His Herculean strength sent
the man stumbling back into his cohort, knocking down the
whole line of men like dominoes. The clattering of course disturbed Walter and his followers who immediately ceased in
their worship. Aware they were now under attack, they pulled
out their swords and readied themselves. Alice and the women
turned to escape along one of the many passages. Henrich had
also unsheathed his sword and now began to hack at those soldiers struggling to stand. They slipped and slid on the muddy
stones, but there was one at the back who had managed to
regain his footing. He still had hold of his crossbow and frantically loaded it, aiming at the forester. In his panic, he missed
his target. The colossal forester felt the wind rush past his ear
and sighed in relief. But then all heard a cry. Henrich dared not
turn to see who was hit, but continued to slash through the
men who stood in his wake. Those soldiers who did not fall to
Henrich's sword turned and ran, tumbling out of that crowded
wet passageway. But as the forester turned round to check on
his charge, he heard they were now singing a song of sorrow.
There, laid out on the stone floor, was Alice de Lud-Auk. The
bolt from the crossbow had hit her in the chest, piercing her
heart and now she was dead. That pathetic shot from the
crossbow had done more damage than any had anticipated.

The saddened party carried Alice's limp body up out of Lud's Church, a princess lifted from a secret cave. And near to that place, they dug a makeshift grave, where they lowered down their precious preacher. Walter stood watching the young men cover his granddaughter with earth, his eyes filling with tears. Alice had been a great hope and joy to him – a living memory of his son but one who would have brought faith to those who would believe. And now that life was gone.

As the old man's tears splashed down onto the red soil and watered that place, he spoke a prayer of thanks for this woman's life. Then he gazed at the fresh mound beside Lud's Church where his hope was buried. Years later a tree would grow over that grave, hiding it from any who would look for Alice's body, obscuring the place where that young female preacher lies.

Now that Lud's Church had been discovered, Walter and his people knew they would have to abandon the place. The soldiers were sure to return, but where should they go now? There was no need to answer that question. The soldiers had returned and brought with them many others. Peaceably then, Walter and his followers, including Henrich Montair, gave themselves up to the authorities. They were led way, taken from their place of worship, taken from their resting preacher – never to return.

No one is sure now exactly where Alice lies up there beside Lud's Church. There are many trees and so her resting place is well and truly hidden. It was to acknowledge Alice de Lud-Auk's presence that Philip Brocklehurst placed a female effigy on a rock shelf up in Lud's Church. For 100 years people would see it and remember the sad story associated with that revered place. The figurehead is gone now and many think of the place simply as a home for fairies, or as a beautiful natural feature.

The amount of people who know of the tragedy that happened there is probably tiny, which is why I tell this story.

SIR GAWAIN AT THE GREEN CHAPEL

The medieval tale of Sir Gawain and the Green Knight is one that entered the English imagination in recent centuries, despite being 700 years old. It has been suggested that it was written by a monk and that the language used is certainly of the region where the three Moorlands counties meet. Each county therefore lays claim to the tale and retells it using locations found within their borders. However, I must admit that Staffordshire looks to have the strongest claim. The unnamed monk who authored the work could very well have been at the abbey located at Dieulacres and used two local sites as inspiration for two key scenes in the work. Sir Bertilak's residence of Hautdesert could very well be Swythamley Hall and the Green Chapel is said to have been inspired by Lud's Church. A visit to this natural feature does summon up those scenes from Sir Gawain's adventure like no other location claiming the accolade. I have therefore retold this tale, focusing it on Lud's Church, where Gawain arrives carrying with him all memories of his adventures thus far.

After one year of searching, the young Knight of the Round Table had finally arrived. Accompanied by the servant of Sir Bertilak, Sir Gawain now stood at the entrance to what he had been told was indeed the Green Chapel. The servant could accompany him no further. His job was done in showing this warrior of Camelot the location of this ancient site. Therefore, with wishes of *bonne aventure* and good providence, he turned his donkey about to leave the young champion to face whatever Fate would bring.

It was one year ago that Sir Gawain had taken up this challenge. It was during Christmastide, when all was merry there in the great hall of Camelot. Knights and their ladies partook of the jollities of that happy season, together with their King and his Queen, the Lady Guinevere. But on one particular night, their carousing was disturbed by the unannounced arrival of the Green Knight, so called for his skin and hair was the colour of the Christmas tree, as well as his armour and even his stead. Yet it was the green-coloured axe, which he carried in his right hand, that summoned the most consternation. Still seated in the saddle in the presence of the King, that Green Knight issued a challenge to all present.

'Whosoever is brave enough to step up and take this axe, then bring it to my neck, will face me where I will do the same to him, one year hence.'

It was Sir Gawain, the youngest member of that brother-hood, who bravely volunteered, knowing that with such an axe he would remove that churlish knight's head from its shoulders and how could he then bring the axe to Gawain's neck, be it in one week or one year?

But when that blade sliced off that Green Knight's head, and when a cheer erupted from the brotherhood, all gasped to see life remaining in that green form, hands reaching to lift up the head. And from those lips came the reminder of this challenge.

'In one year then Sir Gawain, you and I shall meet. Come to me at the Green Chapel where I shall bring this axe to your neck.'

That was one year ago and now Sir Gawain had journeyed to these outlying Moorlands, so far from any road or dwelling, to enter this ancient Green Chapel where he might easily find an end to his few years.

Before he entered that stony sanctuary, Gawain loosened his breastplate and checked that he had hidden there the one thing that might ensure he walked out from that chapel and so ride another day. On his expedition to this godforsaken haunt, Sir Gawain had rested not so far away and enjoyed the warm hospitality of one Sir Bertilak. And it was there at Hautdesert, known to some as Swythamley Hall, with its bustling company, crackling fires and soft, welcoming beds, that Sir Gawain had caught the attentions of Sir Bertilak's lady. And she had given to him one particular gift – a green kirtle.

'This kirtle will turn away any blade,' she had told the young knight in softened tones. 'The wearer will be protected from sword or spear … or axe.'

And so it was this simple keepsake, which Gawain had kept about his person, hidden underneath his armour. He knew the blade that awaited him within the chapel. This green kirtle was all that provided him with some assurance of surviving this fell ordeal. Certain now of its presence then, the knight slid down from his horse, Gringolet. Slowly he tied the horse's reins to the branch of a nearby tree, ensuring no escape; taking time and care over those knots he chose to use, until he could delay no longer. And so he returned to the entrance, a pathway leading between two walls of stone. With hands placed on those rocky pillars, to better steady himself, the knight pushed his way into that hidden world.

Looking about, Sir Gawain saw that he stood in a series of deep trenches, cut into that land by some ancient hand. Light dropped down from the roofless heights, but the grey clouds of that rain-filled day dimmed any cheer such light could give. With walls close either side, damp and dripping, Sir Gawain's hand slipped on green mosses as he sought to steady his

approach. His tripping slowed his progress under those hanging
ferns, which was not unappreciated. He had no desire to race
to his death, but still he must continue. And with each falter-
ing step, the knight felt watched. It was the strange shaping of
overhanging stone catching the light and casting shadows, but
for a second there was a face here gazing down. In one corner he
spied a grimace, in another a screaming mouth, and here two
dark eyes, lifeless and distant.

As the knight stared at these likenesses, looking for any
which resembled his challenger, he slipped again, his feet now
sinking in the red mud below. He pulled his foot from the sucking floor, at once both sinking and tripping – the surface soft

in one place but uneven in another. The blood-coloured dirt splattered over Sir Gawain's armour as he struggled to continue forward and remain upright. But still he ventured deeper into that treacherous chamber. Shadows of confusion began to arrest his mind, as other passages appeared in the rock, some leading to further corridors of stones, creating a network of channels. Others wound away to what Gawain could only imagine were separate chambers, false leads in that perfidious temple.

Till at last he heard a sound to reassure him that his path was true. It was the rasping of a blade against a whetstone. The sound that meant his ordeal was near. And as he turned that corner, he saw the great figure of the Green Knight preparing his axe in this diabolical chapel.

'I have come,' spoke a breathless Sir Gawain, but his words slipped to the ground even as they left his lips. No echo, no life, only death.

The Green Knight saw his arrival and with outstretched arm indicated where the young knight should kneel. Obediently then, Sir Gawain brought his knees to the ground and, removing his helmet, leant his head forward to expose his neck, ready for the blade.

And as that sharpened green metal was raised into the air, Sir Gawain's mind wandered in that moment to when he was, but days ago, a guest at the castle of Sir Bertilak. On his first day at the Castle Hautdesert, his host had told him to rest, but had also set up a bargain between the two: the master would go out to hunt that morning while Sir Gawain remained in the home; whatever each of them received that day they should give to the other. The hunter would bring whatever he had caught and the young knight would present his host with whatever he had gained from within the hall.

The next morning, as he rested in his bed, Sir Gawain was visited by his host's lady. Her interest in the famed knight was great and she slipped purposefully into his bedchamber, locking the door behind her, to welcome him properly with all her charms. Although his heart beat fast within his breast, Sir Gawain resisted all the lady had to offer, save for a single kiss with which she finally bid him farewell that morning.

When Sir Bertilak returned and presented his guest with the meat of a wild boar from the hunt, Sir Gawain presented his host with a single kiss – which surprised the man, but he did not enquire further from where this gift had come.

And now the axe came whistling through the air towards Sir Gawain, who no longer could contain the fear within his chest. Suddenly he flinched, ducking back. And the axe missed him completely.

The Green Knight stared at the knight who had in that second acted with such cowardice. Sir Gawain knew that he must take his place again, wait for the axe to fall a second time and this time let it reach his neck.

And as that sharpened green metal was raised into the air, Sir Gawain's mind wandered in that moment to when he was, but a day or so back, a guest at the castle of Sir Bertilak. The bargain set by his host had carried over into the next day, and when Sir Bertilak had gone out again to hunt that morning, Sir Gawain was once more visited by the lady of the house. Her interest in the famed knight continued and she appeared anew in his bedchamber, this time showing more of her slender form than before. Sir Gawain felt stirrings deep within his being, but remained true to his resolve and so gained that day nothing more than two kisses from the lady.

When Sir Bertilak returned that evening, he presented his guest with the meat of a deer. Sir Gawain dutifully gave his host two kisses, the gifts that he had gained. And the man enquired no further from whence these gifts had come.

And as the axe came whistling through the air towards Sir Gawain, the Green Knight twisted awkwardly and missed the knight, who was knelt resolute and obedient. The Green Knight stared at his axe. Sir Gawain wondered if the green kirtle was working its protection, which was promised by the lady. Yet, Gawain knew the challenge was that the axe should meet his neck and that had not happened. So he remained in his place and waited for the Green Knight to ready himself again.

And as that sharpened green metal was raised into the air a third time, Sir Gawain's mind wandered to when he was, only yesterday, a guest at the castle of Sir Bertilak. Still the bargain set by his host had remained, and when Sir Bertilak had yet again left his castle for the hunt, Sir Gawain had received the lady to his bedchamber a third time. Her charms again caused much perspiration from the knight, but still he resisted. And just when he thought that she would leave, she stopped and her hands wandered silently across her slim frame to the belt, which held fast her robes. Slowly she undid this fastening and slender hand over slender hand pulled out from its loops the soft green kirtle. Then she presented her token, her favour, to Sir Gawain and told him that the simple green silk would turn away any blade. He took that protection from her soft, thin fingers, and she stole three kisses. Then she slid from that bedchamber with a musical laugh lifting the air like the song of the morning lark.

When Sir Bertilak returned that evening, he presented his guest with the tail of a fox. Sir Gawain gave his host three kisses, one of the gifts he had gained that day. And so that young knight dishonoured the agreement made between him and his host, in secret, for he believed that his need for that green kirtle was great.

And as the axe came whistling through the air towards Sir Gawain, it clipped him on his neck and slit the surface of his skin. Blood dripped onto Gawain's knee, but his head remained upon his shoulders. The green kirtle had protected him. In a flash, the knight was to his feet, helmet replaced, shield on his arm and sword in hand. He stood ready to take on that Green Knight should he try to remove his head. The deal was done. The axe had met his neck and still his head remained. But then, before the young knight's eyes, a transformation began. That inhuman warrior changed in shape, becoming more the average height. He lost the green colour from his skin and now, before Sir Gawain, in that dripping trench there stood his host of that past week.

'Sir Bertilak?'

'Yes, indeed,' laughed the generous knight, ''Twas I, all along.'

Bewildered, Gawain lowered his sword and listened as Sir Bertilak explained.

'This was a test, my boy, a challenge to a knight such as yourself. And you have proved yourself as one who is worthy. Under an enchantment, I came to Camelot, seeking you out to take on this trial. Not only did you come to this place to meet the axe, and your likely death, but you passed another test along the way.'

The young knight blushed behind the metal of his helmet, remembering those mornings in his bed, with visits from this knight's wife.

'Aye, I know of this for my wife and I prepared these further trials for you. Yet, fair as my lady is, you resisted her charms a full three times. Not only that, but you presented me with the kisses she gave to you, whenever I returned from the hunt.'

And then the knight's face turned stern and he strode over with resolute steps to Sir Gawain. Before the young knight could discern what action he was to take, Sir Bertilak had slipped his hand behind Gawain's breastplate and quickly pulled out from that screen his lady's kirtle, glistening green in the little light that there was in that place.

'You gave me all, apart from this,' said the elder knight, his voice now booming in the ears of the younger.

In shame, Gawain looked to the floor, his armoured feet covered in mud.

'My apologies Sir Bertilak,' whispered Sir Gawain. 'I am not worthy to sit at the Round Table. I thought more of my own life than of the code of chivalry. My concern was to save my head, and so I kept hold of that which was rightly yours.'

'Indeed you did,' Bertilak's face was like the stone of those surrounding walls, but then he softened. 'Gawain, you are no worse than other men. How many, through fear, choose to save their own life rather than obey an ancient code of manners? You are not the first to choose survival over imposed principles. And so, you have shown yourself to simply be a human.'

Gawain shrugged. These words were of little comfort to him. The knights of Camelot prided themselves on being a higher class of men and he had shown himself to be a simple human.

'Do not be downcast, good Sir Gawain.' Bertilak now placed an encouraging hand upon the young man's shoulder. 'Your head is still on your shoulders and that is not because of the green kirtle. Rather for your chastity and resistance to temptation. My first two swings of the axe missed your neck for these very attributes. The third only nicked your neck for this misdemeanour with the kirtle. Had you fallen for the charms of my lady then be assured that your head would now be lying in the mud and this conversation would be no more than a figment of wishful thinking. You are a man of honour – simply a man with fears and concerns, but one of honour still, Sir Gawain, Knight of the Round Table.'

Gawain brightened slightly and lifted his head to look again at his host.

The two turned to walk out from that enchanted array of stone channels. As they made their way past the moss-covered rocks, Sir Bertilak explained that his wife was in fact the infamous Morgana le Fay, like the fairy folk of those Moorlands, and this was how he had come to be enchanted. He went on to invite Sir Gawain to remain with them for a day or two more at Castle Hautdesert.

'Morgana would like to see you as herself this time. Not in the guise of a knight's young wife, but as your kindly aunt, for she is your Uncle Arthur's half-sister.'

This information did not bring any further comfort to the knight, and as the two passed out of that so-called Green Chapel, and Sir Gawain untied his horse, he thanked his host, but declined the offer.

'They are waiting for me at Camelot,' he said. 'The Knights of the Round Table will want to hear of my adventure and all that has happened in my journey here. Besides, many of them will expect that my head has left my shoulders and so believe I never will return in one piece. I therefore thank you, gracious Bertilak, for all the fine hospitality you have provided for me and I will pass on your regards to the King. However, I will set out on the road home now and hope that one day our paths will cross again.'

And with such kind words, as manners exchanged with no real meaning, the two knights politely separated. Gawain climbed up again onto the back of his faithful steed, Gringolet. And the two began that long road home, returning then to Camelot, to Arthur and his knights, and to that royal lady, Queen Guinevere.

A GRISLY TALE OF GRADBACH

A pedlar was travelling across the moors, but was beaten home by the sun, and so looked for somewhere he might stay for the night. He came across a house set in the woods and found the family there welcomed him in. However, they were not ones for much conversation, and looked him up and down in a curious way every so often. The pedlar was given a tankard of ale, which he welcomed, but again the family members looked at him closely, then nodded to each other. They hurriedly left the room and the pedlar was alone. He decided to sit for a while in a large chair by the fire. He had walked a long way and there, in the half-darkness, the beer and the warmth of the flames were doing their work. He felt a weariness overcome him. His eyelids grew heavy and naturally he began to doze in that wide, welcoming chair. It was just as he was about to drop off into a deep, deep sleep that he heard the creak of the door to the kitchen and a light streamed in. He didn't open his eyes, but remained in the chair, loath to get up or be engaged in any conversation. He could hear the light footsteps of a child moving closer to him and sensed that some-one small was now standing very close. He allowed his eyelids to open slightly and saw in the light a girl who was gazing intently at his hands as they rested on the arms of the chair. And what she said made his hair stand on end.

It was as if she was wondering to herself, but the girl said aloud, 'My, what fat fingers he has. They will make some lovely pies very soon.'

Then, he heard a hiss and the girl obediently ran back to the kitchen door, which was quickly shut behind her.

The pedlar was wide awake now and sat up to see a pair of dogs lying in front of the fire. He had not given them a second thought before, but it now dawned on him that they were there to keep an eye on their master's guest. The two hounds seemed to be asleep, lulled also by the darkness and the fire. Edging himself up carefully, the terrified man tiptoed past the sleeping dogs, letting them lie, hoping to reach the door. Just the click of the catch or the squeak of the hinge would awaken those hairy watchmen. So, gently easing the lock with his pudgy fingers, he slowly opened the door only as far as he needed, slid out silently, and ran. Stumbling over the rough path, which had brought him to this terrifying place, tripping on roots and rocks, he soon came to a bridge, by which he crossed the River Dane. But as he did so he heard the barking of dogs and the shouts of men. Briefly looking back he saw lights moving through the trees and he knew that his would-be captors were on his trail. They were not going to let their next meal get away so easily. In a panic, he fled from the bridge and ran on, guessing at his route under the shining moon. Out there on the moors, he was lost and alone. He had no guide and doubtless these savages knew every inch of this landscape. Soon he stumbled onto a road and could see lights in the distance – houses. Not one lone house, but a street filled with them. It was the village of Gradbach. There, in breathless terror, he banged on doors, screamed for help, until the street was full of people perplexed at such commotion. Hurriedly the pedlar told the gathered folk of what he had escaped. A gang was summoned and whilst the man remained to be cared for, the menfolk of Gradbach marched up and across the bridge to that lone house in the woodland.

They say that the grisly family was captured and all of them were put to death, being hanged in the trees about those moors. The dogs were shot. The house was smashed up and set alight, so that they were rid of whatever grim remains were hidden in that place. But I am not so sure what happened to the little girl. Were the people of Gradbach so frenzied in their actions that the girl was hanged as well? Or did she escape their clutches, being small enough to slip from the grasp of her rough captors? Running into the woodland she disappeared into the shadows under those darkened trees. She heard the yelps of her family dogs being slaughtered. She watched her home go up in flames. And anger burned inside her heart, until her thoughts turned to her stomach. How hungry she was and now she would have to find her own food. So turning from that sorry scene, she headed out onto the moors, wandering over the rocks and hills, looking for anyone who might be on their own. Anyone separated from those they had travelled with. And in her innocence she would approach them, a little girl apparently lost on the moors as well. Together they would walk hand in hand and then she would need a rest. A quiet cave would be nearby, a handy shelter where they could stop for just a few minutes. And there she knew that very soon her dinner would be served.

THE HEADLESS HORSEMAN

It is said that in times gone by a brave knight lived on the moors, but he was called to fight in a furious battle where, with his fellow horsemen, he rode to protect this England. Wrapped in his cloak of gold and carrying an ancient staff, this knight looked a fine and magical figure. Riding high into the fray, he instilled courage in his men and fear in his enemies. And it was in this one last battle that the knight called his men and rode forth deep into the fight, crying out with a rousing voice, his staff in one hand and shining sword held in the other. But on this occasion, his enemy had the upper hand. A well-timed swing of the enemy's blade met with the brave knight's neck. His head was neatly cloven from his shoulders and, flying over the skirmishing foot soldiers, it was lost forever in the melee. That knight remained sitting upright in the saddle, despite the loss of his head. His horse then took off to leave the battle, riding back full speed to its master's home. Galloping over hill and plain, until it came to the Moorlands, that horse careered into the yard where it had always been stabled, its master's body still sat upright on its back. Once at home, that weary steed gave one final snort, which shuddered through its body, and then fell dead upon the ground.

Since that day, some say they have seen that knight, a headless horseman, wandering the moors at night. A gold cloak still hangs about his shoulders and in his hand the staff

remains. The horse is said to float over the ground, its legs frozen so it appears in the action of a gallop; like that from a fairground carousel perhaps. But it is not for fun that this horse materialises. This apparition has come to be known as a harbinger of death.

There is a tale of a man who was riding home across the moors very late one evening. And as his horse trotted down a lane, his dog gently running alongside, a knight on a horse suddenly came up behind them and fell in beside the rider. He had heard tell of the headless horseman and kept his eyes forward, choosing to ignore this dreadful companion. Maybe he thought that it would go away. But as they continued along the lane, he could see out of the corner of his eye, the horseman raising his staff to point at the man and a chill ran through his body. Clipping his horse's side with his heels, he quickened his pace to outride the menacing escort and to his surprise left that worrying rider behind. He continued his hastened pace until he was sure the horseman had gone, and eventually he was home. He leapt off his horse and rushed indoors to tell his wife of his traumatic ride. Now, even though some had said that a meeting with this headless horseman would mean death, that rider had no trouble with his own health as a result of this encounter. Instead, it was the horse and dog, for both died within a few days. Although sad to have lost two faithful friends, the man counted himself lucky to have survived that evil day at all.

And then there was one who was not so fortunate. The story goes that another man was heading home late one evening. He was walking this time and wondered how he might get home more quickly. It was as he was considering the possibility of a shortcut that there was a sudden rush of wind and the man was lifted from the ground. Shouting and struggling, he found himself being whisked through the Moorlands at a great rate, through wooded land and over bushes, flying past rocky outcrops and splashing into streams and rivers. He could feel an arm holding him fast and how he was sat on something, his legs dangling either side. And slowly, through the frenetic flight, he realised that he was on the back of a horse and in the clutches of a knight with no head. Screaming now in fear, the man was carried for many miles, the headless horseman continuing his mysterious run to the man knew not where. Until finally, that frightened man was flung from the horse and the headless horseman flew away into the night. Breathless and confused that poor man rose to his feet and heard a voice calling him. It was his wife, for he had been thrown down at the front door of his home. He had earlier wanted to find a shortcut home, but that terror-filled flight with the headless horseman was not what he had hoped for. Still haunted by the memories of such an ordeal, the man went to bed, but he could not sleep. Reliving those wild and perilous miles, he sat up screaming in his bed. Until finally his fragile mind and body could take it no longer, and the man was dead.

The Mermaid of Blackmere

There was once a man who went to sea and returned to live on the moors of Staffordshire. Many people bring back a trinket or two from their travels, a curiosity perhaps. Others find the love of their life, bringing them back to their home to meet family and friends. It could be said that this sailor found both, for he brought back with him a mermaid. Now many legends tell of how a mermaid's tail can be transformed into a pair of legs to enable her to move about freely in the land of humans. This was not true for this particular lady of the sea. Her fishy tail remained whether she was on land or in the water. The sailor then had to find somewhere for his love to stay and, having purchased a house in Morridge, brought her to Blackmere, a tarn not so far from where he lived. He would come down to the mere each day and together the two would talk and laugh and even swim together. In the evenings, they would look out across the landscape, which dropped away, bounding off into hills and heathland, painted purple and pink by the setting sun. These were precious times they shared together and, with the company of her loved one, the mermaid was able to tolerate the confines of the mere. She was of course used to the unending openness of the ocean, but as long as the sailor was with her each day she was able to make the best of living in that dark pool, off the side of a lonely road.

However, such relationships between humans and immortals will always end in sadness. The time came when age caught up with the sailor and he died. The two lovers had allowed no one else in to their relationship as they felt they had all they needed in each other. But now, with no friends or family members, the mermaid realised how she was in fact trapped, destined to remain in Blackmere for the rest of her days, which would be many, many more.

As each year passed, the mermaid became more and more frustrated. She finally cursed the day she had met that man who had brought her here. The sailor had certainly been a bit of a loner. All that time he had spent alone with his love, telling no one of his secret, meant that none of the precious few people who did venture up to the mere knew that a mermaid resided below in its dark waters.

That is until a farmer decided that he would drain the mere, so as to make better use of the land. He brought his men to the edge of the tarn to discuss how best to drain this useless body of water. Yet as they talked the surface of the water began to bubble. Someone had been listening in to their conversation and she was not going to let them take away what little water she did have. These humans only considered themselves. She had decided therefore to give them something to truly think about. A wave of fury swooped through the water and crashed onto the shore, soaking the startled farm hands. And up from the mere arose one enraged mermaid. 'How dare you even consider taking the one body of water I have to live in!' she hissed. Then she spat this curse at the farmer.

'If you should drain this mere, know that the nearby dwelling of humans, the one you call Leek, will be drowned in the very water you take from this place. The people there will discover a new reason for its name before they die, and it will be your fault!'

The farmer and his men were so frightened by the irate mermaid that they ran back to the farm, pushing and shoving each other in their efforts to be as far from that that seething creature as possible. None of them thought of draining that mere again. Yet, it seems the fear the watery maiden instilled was so strong that now no bird is ever seen resting on the water, and no animal will come near it to drink. The mermaid waits below the water, her rage growing with every passing year. The birds of the air and creatures of the land sense her anger and so avoid the water. They know that if they flutter down or draw too near, a wiry hand will reach out to pull them in and to their deaths.

THE BLACK CAT OF GETLIFFE'S YARD

There were two women who lived side by side and generally got on well. One was a baker, whilst the other was known for being a fortune-teller. This second woman had a black cat, which liked to wander about the houses and shops of Getliffe's Yard. It would weasle its way in through open windows and squeeze past doors left ajar. Then it would help itself to whatever scraps had been left out. The cat sometimes would, if it was lucky, find an uncovered jug of milk, but in its eagerness the beast would often knock that jug to the floor. The smash, as it hit the floor, would alert the owner, who would come running and see the culprit just as it escaped the way it had come. That black cat had quickly become unpopular with the locals and, despite their efforts to keep the windows and doors closed, it kept on appearing.

One day the baker woman was cooking up a batch of oatcakes when, who should appear in her bakery? The black cat. She did not want that creature getting anywhere near her batch of mix and so she tried hissing at the cat. That didn't work, so she tried shooing it away. That didn't work, so she tried lifting it and putting it outside. But, every time she turned her back, the cat reappeared. The baker woman did not have time for this and immediately lost her temper with that impertinent intruder. In a fury, she threw at the cat a tray of hot cakes, which had just come from the oven. The poor creature was hit and scalded. Crying out, it ran from the bakery, its mews of pain being heard even though it had gone beyond the door. Instantly, the baker woman was sorry for what she had done. The cat was obviously in pain and she had not meant to hurt it. She ran out of the bakery and round to her neighbour's house where she knew the cat lived.

The door was open and so, without a thought, the baker woman went straight in. And there she saw her neighbour getting up from the floor half-dressed. Her black dress was about her body but not pulled up, so that her back was revealed. The baker woman gasped, first because she had disturbed her neighbour, who appeared to be getting dressed, but then again because she saw on the woman's back a large burn in much the same place that the black cat had been hit by the scalding hot oatcakes.

When the baker woman told her customers what she had seen, they all nodded. She had only affirmed what they had been thinking. That troublesome black cat was in fact the fortune-teller, who was clearly a witch, able to transform herself at will. Some were scared to hear such things, but others thought that her fortune-telling must have been accurate, surmising that if she had the power to change her form then she must have powers to read the future. And I daresay that, in the end, that shape-shifting woman benefited from receiving a tray of hot oatcakes to the back.

THE WANDERING JEW

Tales of the Wandering Jew have been retold all over Europe as this mysterious figure makes his lonely way from village to town to city; he is constantly dying of thirst, but knows that his life shall not end. He curses the day that he found himself some 2,000 years ago in Jerusalem, caught up with the crowds gathered on the day that Christ was sentenced to death. Standing at the front of the masses, Jesus stumbled in front of this Jewish man; the Lord, gasping, asked for water. The Hebrew had no idea who the man was, only that he had been sentenced to crucifixion and so he must be a criminal. He therefore felt all the hatred rise up in him from years of oppression by the Roman forces and struck the pathetic man across the face. Those about him laughed as they saw the weak, helpless figure hit the floor in the dust.

'Go on, go on,' laughed the man. 'What are you hanging about for?'

As Jesus slowly lifted his face from the stony ground, blood again dripping from his lips, he whispered something to that man. Something about those eyes stopped the man's laughter and now he was stilled. Leaning forward, he heard those words uttered by Christ. 'I will go. I will go on, but you will wait for my return.'

The man wanted to dismiss this as the mutterings of a madman. Why should he wait for this wretch to come back? He was to be put to death on a cross. So the man gathered his purple robe about him and walked away from the crowds.

Some say this man was called Ahasver, others have different names for him, but whatever his name may have been, that scene there, outside Pilate's Hall of Justice, played on his mind, even into old age. Maybe death would finally release him from those haunting images, those lingering words. But it seems there was more to those words than Ahasver could ever have imagined, for death did not come. Those people he had known as a child passed away, and he still lived. He saw children, grandchildren and great-grandchildren grow up and die and he still lived. Empires fell and new kings rose up, and still he lived. His years were now no more than one long series of goodbyes. How many more must he befriend and then finally bury? The continual round of welcomes, friendships and then departures grew too much for his heart. He would rather have no friends than have to say goodbye again.

So began a life of moving on. Like Cain of old, he became a restless wanderer on the earth. And some say he roams the globe with an insatiable thirst, a reminder of Christ's own situation when he asked this Ahasver for a cup of water. This man must wander until the end of time, for Jesus told him that he would 'wait until my return'. Who knows when the Second Coming is to be?

It has been 2,000 years now and many have claimed to have met this Wandering Jew. Books and plays have been written about him. He must have trodden over many thousands of miles. And it is said that he was even seen on the Staffordshire Moorlands.

There was a lame man who lived in a small cottage on his own in the Moorlands. I presume he must have had people to help him, bringing the food he needed for instance. But I do know that he liked to brew his own beer. This made sense, as it was not easy for him to get along to the pub.

One evening there was a knock at the door. The Staffordshire man called out for whomever it was to come in, and through the door stepped an elderly stranger dressed in a long purple robe. He asked in a rasping voice if there was anything here to drink. He was on a journey and was so thirsty. The Staffordshire man could hear this in his voice, which was like a stone being dragged over a desert. He told the stranger he was most welcome to have a jug of beer, but he would need to help himself as he couldn't get about quick enough and the stranger might die of thirst before he managed to pour him a drink. The stranger mumbled something about 'Chance would be a fine thing' but then thanked the man and came full into the house to take a drink from the barrel. The Staffordshire man tried to engage the stranger in conversation. He didn't get out much and so he liked to know what was going on out and about, even if he only heard about the weather. But the stranger didn't want to talk and was savouring the beer anyway.

When he finally finished, the stranger thanked the man and reached into a leather bag, which hung from his shoulder. He pulled out a handful of leaves and suggested that the man steep two or three of them in the beer each time he took a mugful.

'Do this for about two weeks,' he said. 'You'll find it'll do wonders for you.'

Then the stranger slipped out of the door and was never seen again.

The Staffordshire man thought he'd give it a try, although he wasn't sure what leaves they were. Each time he had a mug of beer he steeped a few leaves in it, just as instructed.

It was about two weeks later that he began to find feeling in his toes. A few days more and he could move his legs. A few weeks later his strength had returned. And finally the Staffordshire man was able to get up and walk about. So he got himself dressed, marched down to the local pub and told them the story of the thirsty stranger and his healing leaves.

Meanwhile, Ahasver knew it would not be long until he was thirsty again. He had to keep on moving. He did not want to make friends and he did not want to be asking the same people for a drink. He turned east and headed off with his purple cloak wrapped tight about him. He would soon reach the town of Stamford, where others would later tell of his appearance.

EVANGELIST TO THE MOORLANDS

Being a resident of Cheshire, I know St Bertram better as St Berteline, but then others spell it St Bertoline. He has also been known as St Bartholomew and Becceline. I like to call him Bert, which works for most people. It was this oft-forgotten saint, truly local to Mercia, who eventually became the patron of Stafford. He had a bit of a false start, being a runaway prince who wanted to follow in St Patrick's footsteps and take the Gospel to Ireland. It was, however, there that he met a beautiful princess and his calling was quickly forgotten. The two were secretly married, but had to escape from Ireland. Returning to Britain with his bride, Bert found that he was no longer welcome in the kingdom of Mercia, having offended his father when he cast away his royal position so indifferently. The ex-prince and his ex-princess therefore wandered the bleak Moorlands of Derbyshire and Staffordshire, until tragedy struck. Bert's young bride was killed by wolves whilst sheltering in Thor's Cave at Wetton. This was followed by an encounter with the Devil himself. Although Bert managed to see off th'Olde Lad, he recognised how much he was lacking as a holy man again – a good place to start afresh, perhaps.

One particular holy man came to mind as Bert considered where he should go next. His name was Guthlac and he had been a soldier serving under Bert's own father. He remembered hearing when he was a boy how Guthlac had denied his successes as the King's warrior, turned his back on fighting and had become a monk at Repton. Then he had moved off to a dark and watery place outside of the kingdom: Crowland in the Fens. Bert thought that if anyone was to understand his situation, then it would likely be Guthlac. Even though this holy man had not been a prince, he knew what it was to give up privilege and position, and what it was to court the King's displeasure. Bert decided then that he would go to Guthlac, to join his brotherhood and learn from him. And so began the long journey of some 100 miles to find this man and ask him to be his mentor.

Travelling along the edge of the Peak District, the cold harsh winds beating about his face, the young ex-prince shivered in his thin, torn robes. He considered how he had been so expectant of his mission to Ireland and how he now had great expectations of Crowland. Maybe he should not expect too much. The winds continued to howl about and Bert thought that, in this strange landscape, he could hear voices. Distant howls and cries coming from over the hills or behind the wind-formed rocky sculptures. Sometimes the howls reminded him of the wolves and that terrible night outside Wetton. Other times he was sure he could hear a voice whispering something over and over.

'Grassssp what is yoursssss,' it seemed to say. 'Grassssp what is yoursssss.'

Well, that was what he was attempting to do, wasn't he? He had made up his mind to seek out Guthlac. He was taking hold of his life again. So with these words echoing about him, Bert strode on.

It took a lot longer to find Guthlac than Bert had first thought. He had asked at this church and that abbey, until finally he came to the wet, boggy lands of the Fens. Splashing his way through the marshes, his feet soggy and smelly, he finally saw a mound rising up from the dank landscape. It was an ancient burial mound – could this really be the place?

As Bert approached the mound, a shape suddenly rose up like a spirit warding off all who would rob its grave. Bert stumbled back and his foot sank again into the stinking mud.

'And who might you be?' spoke the shape, silhouetted against the setting sun, which seemed to have given up the fight to shine in this misty, mosquito-ridden land.

'My name is Berteline,' answered the traveller, 'I was a prince of Mercia once.'

The shape clambered over the mound and moved towards Bert, like a shadow in strange robes. As it approached, Bert could see it was a man, but covered in a garment made of animal skins, some of the fur still remaining, but wet and matted.

'So it is!' spoke the wild man with surprise. 'It is indeed Berteline; Prince Berteline, in fact. But no longer prince, you say?'

'You are Guthlac?' Bert asked. This wasn't quite what he imagined the holy man to be.

'I am. Welcome, Berteline, to my place of retreat. Come in and tell me what brings you out to these forsaken reaches of your father's kingdom.'

Slipping and sliding, Bert clambered up onto the mound and followed this unusual holy man into the chamber, which had been emptied and made into a dwelling of sorts.

'I can only offer you some barley bread. Perhaps a bit of fish,' said Bert's holy host.

'But then the pleasures of the flesh are what I have denied. Resist the demons, my boy. Resist the demons.'

Bert nodded to show agreement.

'Still,' continued Guthlac, 'bread and fish was good enough for the 5,000, so it will sustain me.'

The holy man reached into a wooden box to pull out a small, hard loaf of bread and handed it to his guest. Bert received it politely, but the bread reminded him of some stones he had seen not so long ago. Guthlac then reached up for some fish, which had been hanging over the remains of a small fire, smoking in the mist. Pulling off a few pieces of the hardened flesh, he handed this to Bert, saying, 'Not too much. There's 5,000 to feed remember.'

Bert attempted a smile and then attempted to eat.

'Oh, I nearly forgot,' Guthlac added, and handed over a wooden cup, 'Join me in a small cup of muddy water after sunset.'

Bert took it and sighed. Why did nothing go quite as he imagined?

So began a long, steep – and damp – learning curve for ex-prince Bert. Under the discipleship of Guthlac, Bert met the weird and the wonderful, all of whom managed to make their way out to that forsaken mound in the Fens. Everyone that turned up was as mad as this wild man master, and they all must have had a serious lack of taste buds. Bert learnt how to live with mosquito bites. He learnt how to make wet clothes a little less damp. And he learnt how to nibble a smoked fish to make it last forty days and forty nights. But it was when it came to night that Bert really began to wonder why he stayed with Guthlac. His spiritual father had ensured that in that muddy, smoky burial mound of a cell, he had a decent bed for himself. It was a little damp, but it had a sturdy wooden structure and so was off the ground. Bert, meanwhile, had to sleep on the floor; what there was of it. He had a length of sacking to use as an under blanket, but that did not stop the moisture from rising up into his bones. His pillow at least was dry, but that was because it was a stone – a smooth one. Each night, Bert alternated between shivering due to the clammy conditions and having an aching neck from his head being propped up on a boulder. And he would look at that wild man, sleeping snuggly in his bed – off the ground. Bert sighed, remembering all the stupid mistakes he had made and resigned himself to these conditions, feeling he probably deserved them anyway. A breeze would then drift over the Fens, slithering through the grasses and gathering in strength with each moment. As Bert lay there he thought he could hear that voice again, whispering as he lay looking at the sleeping Guthlac.

Night after night, Bert would lie on the floor watching the slumber of his master, wishing he was in that bed. And each night the breeze seemed to come across the Fens.

'Grassssp what is yoursssss,' it would always say. 'Grassssp what is yoursssss.'

A day then came when Guthlac made a strange request of Bert. It wasn't to wash his clothes in the muddy waters again. Nor was it to make a smoked fish sandwich with a hard stale barley loaf. Instead, Guthlac wanted a shave and asked that Bert be his barber. Bert was surprised that someone who seemed to have no great concern over his appearance should now be asking for a shave. Those who came to this mound in search of a holy man didn't seem to worry about Guthlac's appearance. But he was insistent.

Bert therefore began to boil some water – once he had managed to convince some damp twigs to catch light. And as he waited for the water to boil, he looked at the blade Guthlac had passed to him. It was surprisingly clean and sharp. How did such a man manage to keep *this* in such good nick, when he seemed to have no concern for healthy eating or sanitary living conditions? To Bert it seemed to be yet another example of the inconsistencies of the man.

The water eventually boiled and Bert prepared Guthlac's beard for a shave. He took the blade and began to gently scrape at the bristles, gradually removing the beast-like covering. And as Guthlac sat back, eyes closed, facing Heaven, Bert noticed that a breeze was again slithering through the grasses of that marshland.

'Grassssp what is yoursssss.' he heard a voice whisper again. 'Grassssp what is yoursssss.'

Bert wasn't sure what the voice was talking about, but he could hear it every time he slid the blade over his master's throat.

'Grassssp what is yoursssss. Grassssp what is yoursssss.'

His eye caught the bed in which Guthlac slept every night whilst he spent the night in the wet, his head on a stone.

'Grassssp what is yoursssss. Grassssp what is yoursssss.'

Again, the blade slid over the throat of Guthlac. And Bert wondered what if he should slip? The master's life was at the mercy of his pupil, his head in Berteline's hands and his throat exposed. A mishap with this blade and his master would be dead. Bert would have a bed; he could sleep a little more; more like a prince.

'Grassssp what is yoursssss.'

No one else was here and the marshes would welcome his master's body. It would sink down into the bog, never to be found again.

'Grassssp what is yoursssss.'

And as Bert reached over again to his master, holding the blade a little more tightly, he heard another voice.

'Listening to the Devil's temptations are we, Berteline?'

The ex-prince stopped. It was Guthlac.

'Surprised that I know what you have decided to do?' his master asked, eyes still closed, looking up to Heaven.

Overcome with shame, Bert dropped the blade.

'How did you know?' he whispered.

'I hear the voices of demons, Berteline. And I know the voice of the Father of Lies.' Guthlac then opened his eyes and sat up, turning to look at the guilt-ridden Berteline. 'I have heard that voice every night and so I decided to ask you to give me a shave; to see what you would do.'

Bert fell to his knees. He had failed the test and words of deep apology and repentance tumbled from his lips.

Guthlac then stood up and placed his hand on the head of his disciple. 'Now you are ready to learn,' he said.

From that day on, Bert's time with Guthlac greatly changed. The master told Bert to pack his things and the two of them left the Fens for a trip back to the Staffordshire Moorlands. Guthlac explained that Bert was now ready to return to those bleak hills for a time. There they would visit the people spread out across these high, sparse lands. Guthlac assured Bert that he would always be by his side here. 'There are demons who hide in the rocks all over these Moorlands, Berteline,' he explained. 'But I speak their language and will hear them if any plan to tempt you again.'

Bert thanked his master.

'Yes,' continued Guthlac, 'their words are similar to that of the ancient Britons who first peopled these lands.' He added, 'Their ways were somewhat demonic anyway.'

So, with Guthlac to protect him, Bert set off across the unwelcoming Moorlands, seeking to bring the Gospel to the people there, bringing healing and peace as it was needed. In this way Bert became known as the Evangelist to the Moorlands, as celebrated at St Bartholomew's Church in Longnor. Maybe this was his church at one time, but here he is shown as St Bertram, another name, but that's another story.

3

TALES FROM MERCIAN STAFFORDSHIRE

It was in July 2009 that a great collection of Anglo-Saxon treasure was uncovered in Hammerwich. Known as the Staffordshire Hoard, this discovery helped to renew interest in the Saxon history of the county. In those days, Staffordshire sat pretty much in the middle of the kingdom of Mercia, and, much like today, people passed in and out, crossing back and forth, on military campaigns, trade routes and later following paths of pilgrimage. Some of the great heroes of that time rode through these lands, whether they were mighty warriors seeing off the Danes, or saints slowly transforming the ways of the Saxon people. Those were times of violent change, with not only threats from invaders, but the old ways of pagan worship being challenged and rifts ripping through families and whole communities. Christianity was gradually influencing the kingdom as missionaries and converts worked tirelessly to teach harsh rulers about the Prince of Peace. However, the ways of peace were a long way off as kings and queens, whether Christian or pagan, had to protect these lands from the continual attacks. Saxon Staffordshire then was a fearsome place, but one with hope. Victories were won and protection increased as Alfred the Great's vision of a united England under one ruler slowly drew near. Finally, it was achieved, but not under a Saxon king. That one ruler was Danish, the mighty King Cnut. Such is the irony of history.

This fascinating time period has given us some terrific stories, tales full of inspiration and explanations for how things have come to be. All, from our twenty-first-century standpoint, are enacted by some wonderfully eccentric heroes.

TALE OF ST MODWEN

There was once a holy woman, a princess from Ireland, named Modwen. She was the daughter of King Mochta, the King of Connaught; being the head of a Christian family, he gave his Modwen full support as she prepared to go on pilgrimage to Rome. Crossing the Irish Sea with her two companions, Lazar and Althea, they landed at Holyhead on Anglesey. Then following the pilgrim's way through Wales and into England, they soon walked along the River Trent. It was here that Modwen saw an island and she happened to mention to her companions that it looked to be a good place to build an abbey.

As they journeyed further down the river, they saw many women working in the fields and outside of their homes, and they stopped to talk with them. They heard of the terrible conditions in which many of them lived: deaths during childbirth and bleedings which brought others to early graves. Modwen's heart went out to these women and she could think of little else as she travelled down to Canterbury, across to France and finally on to Rome. It was in this revered city that she made a vow, to serve the women she had met by the River Trent.

It was on their return journey that Modwen, Lazar and Althea stopped at the little island they had discussed before. Naming it Andressey – St Andrew's Isle – Modwen made a home and began to build a chapel. A message was sent home to her father, and whilst she waited for Mochta to send money and workers, Modwen looked at how to enable her little community to survive. They soon found a fresh water spring, which was invaluable to their existence, and so, transforming it into a well, Modwen's community quickly became established. Mochta's men soon arrived and the building work was escalated, meaning that it was really no time at all until a new abbey was standing on Andressey, and the ministry began serving those women who lived thereabouts.

Many of them had to work when they were pregnant, which was not uncommon. It takes all hands to keep a farm turning over. So, Modwen provided two very simple solutions. Firstly, the stick she had used on her long pilgrimage. She would lend this to any woman who needed something to lean on. And when the stick was on loan? Well, Modwen had purchased a sturdy red cow. The beast knew the lot of a mother and was a strong support, something to lean on when out in the fields. So, many came to Andressey for help and spiritual guidance, as well as for healing. Modwen had discovered that the waters from her well could bring about miracles. When she washed the eyes of those who had trouble with their sight, all became clear and they could see again. News of such things quickly spread and many came, bringing elderly relatives and blind children, and many received back their sight.

Word of Modwen's well reached the ears of a hermit who stayed in a cave outside of Breedon, some 15 miles away. He felt great concern for Modwen. She would surely be dealing with endless crowds of people asking for help and healing. When would she have time for herself – for reflection and prayer? And so he set out to Andressey, and, crossing over the river, he met with the young abbess. Taking her to one side, he said that he would come each day and share with Modwen from the writings of the lives of the saints. She eagerly agreed and so began a regular ritual. With prayer and meditation led by the hermit, she was encouraged in her faith and inspired by the examples of those saints' lives of which he read. These meetings nurtured a strong and sustaining relationship for both Modwen and the hermit, enabling them both to grow in their allotted ministries.

It was on one of these occasions that the hermit arrived at Andressey to discover that he had not brought his book with him. Modwen had come to appreciate the readings from this book so much that she sent two young women to go back and fetch the book because the hermit was too old to walk there and back again.

The two set out in a boat up the river, but as they did so a strong wind started up. Rain began to fall, the wind rocked the boat and the waters became increasingly choppy. Full of fear, the girls were at a loss as to what they should do and in their panic overturned the boat. Falling into the water, the boat flipped over and covered the two of them. Then the boat and girls all disappeared under the water and did not resurface.

As time went by, the winds did not seem to be abating and Modwen and the hermit grew increasingly worried about the two they had sent out on such a treacherous trip. Modwen was distraught and believed that the girls must have been drowned. She blamed herself for being so eager to hear of the lives of other saints, that she had forgotten about the safety of those who were in her care. What was the point of being inspired by those from the past when you treated those in the present with such disregard?

The hermit tried to console Modwen and encouraged her to pray. That was all they could do for now. In her fear, Modwen prostrated herself on the ground, weeping and crying out to God to save those poor souls, repenting of her ways and pleading for mercy.

As her cries and tears increased, the hermit grew worried for Modwen and tried to calm the distressed young woman. She was so caught up in her anxiety that she did not even feel the kind hand on her shoulder as the hermit wondered how he could bring her out of this state. He was increasingly concerned for her health. Then, suddenly, the sharp resonant sound of a bell rang out. It was not the chapel bell, but seemed to emanate from out of the sky; resounding through the cell where the two prayed. It shook through their bodies. This heavenly pealing caught Modwen's soul and she immediately stopped weeping. She rose to her feet and gasped. Through the window of the cell, she could see the waters between Andressey and the riverbank. They were dividing to reveal a path. Not a path leading to the bank, but one which ran parallel to it, leading off in the direction that those two young women had taken earlier that day. The wind had calmed, the rain stopped and the sun now shone through the clouds, lighting this path for Modwen and the hermit. The two of them rushed out of the cell and down onto that illuminated lane, neither speaking of what they hoped they would see.

The path led them towards the village of Leigh, where they saw on the now-dry riverbed an upturned boat. It was a curious site, seeing a boat there with the water still flowing either side of it.

As they drew closer, Modwen gasped and pointed. She could see the fingers of the girls protruding out from under the boat, still grasping its sides. Immediately, the hermit ran over and tried to lift the boat, but it was stuck to the ground as if it had grown roots and was now fixed to that riverbed. Stepping back, huffing and puffing, the hermit gladly allowed Modwen to try. Stooping down she stroked the fingers which still clung to the boat. They were like the legs of a crab trapped under a pot. Kneeling there she whispered her apologies to the girls. The fingers twitched. Modwen instinctively reached out with her own fingers, and slid them under the wood of the gunwale. The boat lifted slightly; her hand was now underneath and, with one push, Modwen threw the boat up onto its stern to reveal the two girls. What praises tumbled from her lips as the young abbess saw those in her charge tumble out onto the floor alive and well, if a little shaken. As she hugged the girls and they all marvelled at the miracle that had taken place, the hermit suddenly called out, 'The waters! They are returning! Quick, into the boat!'

And as the miraculous pathway was covered again by the river, the four leapt into the boat. They did not need oars, for a current carried them back to Andressey. Mysteriously the boat stopped at the holy island and the amazed foursome clambered out to tell their story to those awaiting their return.

Modwen's fame and the reputation of her abbey grew and her community eventually developed into the town we now know as Burton-on-Trent. Of course, the time came when she had to leave the earth. When she died, all the women of Burton

were gathered there. In tears, those sisters in Christ bade farewell to the woman who had cared for them, their daughters
and their granddaughters. And as the life slipped from her
aged body, some who knelt there gasped. For up from the
River Trent flew a pair of swans, their feathers silver and shining in the moonlight. The swans passed ethereally through the

abbey walls and were met in the air by Modwen's spirit. Then, as her guides, those silver swans led the soul of the well-loved abbess up, through the abbey roof and to Heaven itself. Some say that it was not two swans, but one. Others say it was more incredible still, being a single swan but with two necks. But this kind-hearted woman, who found the well on Andressey, giving refreshment and healing water to those who came to her, soon became the patron saint of Burton. Its brewers saw themselves as continuing her work, especially those who served under the sign of The Swan with Two Necks.

THE STORY OF STONE

In the misty days of Mercia, there was a king named Wulfhere. He was a proud and powerful man who took his inspiration from his god, Thor. To him, the god of thunder represented power and justice. His anger rolled out across the skies and those who failed him were struck dead by the bolts of lightning that emanated from the heavy strikes of his anvil. That was a god to follow, thought Wulfhere, a mighty lord and fearsome warrior.

Now, it was Wulfhere's desire to unite the kingdoms of Mercia and Kent under his throne and so increase his power. But, there was one problem. The daughter of the King of Kent was very choosy about whom she would marry. Princess Ermenilda was a Christian and had made it very clear that she would not even consider marrying a pagan. This put Wulfhere in a precarious position. The kingdom of Mercia was not powerful enough to subdue the kingdom of Kent and, besides, should the Saxons really be fighting amongst themselves when they had enough trouble keeping off invaders from other lands?

Despite Wulfhere's own vision of himself as Thor's representative on earth, he had learnt that, at times, subtlety was also an effective way to get what you wanted, especially when dealing with women. And so, Wulfhere went to ask for the hand of Ermenilda, claiming that he was a Christian king. His ruse worked and the King of Mercia returned to his throne at Bury Bank with a new Queen to sit beside him. He was now the ruler of both Mercia and Kent, and felt the power of the position coursing through his veins – he was truly the son of Thor. Once back in his own kingdom, Wulfhere revealed to Ermenilda his true religious affiliations and, although shocked, there was not much that the queen could do about it.

The royal family of Mercia and Kent soon grew, as Ermenilda gave birth to three children. She was insistent that they should be brought up as Christians, but Wulfhere disagreed. The two discussed the issue with many raised voices and tears, but both were resolute, until they finally came to a solution. There was one girl and two boys. Ermenilda would bring up the girl, Werburgh, in the ways of Christ, whilst Wulfhere would train the boys, Wulfad and Rufin, to live as he did, for Thor. This proved initially to be a sensible arrangement. Ermenilda would teach her daughter how to be a woman in the royal court anyway, and so could easily council Werburgh in Christian ways. Wulfhere would guide his sons in matters of warfare and hunting, and so pass on to Wulfad and Rufin his obedience to Thor.

The boys grew up into fine warriors and Werburgh into a caring and gracious princess, and their parents agreed that their plan had worked. However, there came a day when the two young princes were out hunting. A white hart had been seen in the woods and they were determined to kill it.

Hurtling through the trees on horseback, Wulfad and Rufin chased their elusive quarry through the forest. It made a break over an open field, but the boys were not quick enough with their arrows. The deer reached the cover of trees again but the princes were on its tail. It was in this wooded glade that they thought they had lost their prey, and as they slowed their horses, the hooves gently padding on the pine-covered floor, Rufin saw a flash of white ahead of them. Silently indicating to his brother, each of them eased out an arrow to load their bows. Taking careful aim and pulling on the string, they were ready to see whose eye was better, when a cry of 'Hold!' startled them. The hart leapt and was gone. The princes' arrows shot ineffectually into the trees, whilst their horses jostled and gazed about. The young men looked up to their left; there, standing before the entrance of a cave, was a man in long, worn robes. They were both angry that such a clear shot had been taken from them, but they did not have the same fire in their bellies as their father. And so they calmed slightly when the stranger apologised and offered the two princes food and drink.

After climbing down from their horses and tying them up, the brothers climbed the small hill to the cave. There they joined the man, who furnished them with a humble but welcome offering of bread, fish and wine.

'I am sorry to have spoilt your fun, dear princes,' the man again said, 'but I believe your presence here in these woods is not a mistake.'

The two young men looked at each other and the stranger continued, 'I was praying here when I heard a voice telling me that you would come, chasing a white hart. But I was told to call you into my humble dwelling and tell you of another whom you hunt, a quarry which has proved more elusive to you, but welcomes you to his heart.'

The words of the stranger were mysterious indeed and although they did not entirely understand what he was talking about, Wulfad and Rufin were enjoying the food and decided to listen more.

Their host went on to introduce himself as Chad, a holy man they had heard of through conversations with their sister, though she had been forbidden from saying more. Now here they were, in his secluded cave. Being a Christian holy man, Chad told a story that had been banned from the princes by their father. It was a tale of sacrifice and forgiveness, a tale which touched the hearts of the two brothers, and did so with such depth that this meeting turned out to be the first of many in the shadow of that sandstone roof. Each day, Wulfad and Rufin would please their father by declaring their desire to go out hunting. They would be gone for much of the day, but never seemed to return with as much as their father had hoped. Of course, their hunt was now not for a physical quarry, but rather chasing what the Celtic Christians referred to as the wild goose, the Holy Spirit of Christ. And so, in their desire for the truth, the royal brothers cloaked themselves in a deception, following their father's footsteps in many ways but in the opposite direction. And it was not long until this secret pathway led the brothers from Chad's cave to his well at Lichfield, where they were baptised, sealing themselves as Christ's own in a covert declaration.

Now, during this time, the sister of the princes, Werburgh, had not been forgotten. In fact, her beauty had caught the attention of one of her father's greatest warriors, a bold pagan man by the name of Werbode. He wished to marry the princess, but was scuppered. She had taken the same decision as her mother, in that she would only marry a Christian.

Werbode was a fine warrior, one who was used to victory, and he did not take easily to being rejected by Werburgh. He tried entreating her, saying that if their gods were not similar then their names, Werburgh and Werbode, were alike, and so the two of them were fated to be together. Werburgh, of course, did not fall for such things, calling them foolishness and repeating her conditions.

'Then I will change!' declared Werbode. But Werburgh knew she could not trust this man's heart. Her mother had been careful to tell her daughter the whole story of her father's dishonesty. So Werbode took to ordering the princess to marry him, hoping, like many men, that his anger would push her to change her mind.

To this, Werburgh responded, 'Foolish is the man who tries to push a woman into his will by anger. What will it lead to but fear and sadness?' And so the furious Werbode stomped off, out of the castle and into the woods, kicking every stone and fir cone which lay in his path.

After an hour or two of wandering and muttering, the rejected suitor came to an unexpected slope in the woods. He lost his footing and slipped. Sliding down the hillside, he was stopped by a low wall of sandstone, which rose up from the ground before him. Pleased his humiliating fall had been interrupted, but not happy to be bruised by crashing into the stone, he was about to begin cursing the hill and the sky and that obstinate princess again, when he heard voices. He was sure he recognised them, but where were they? Carefully rising, he crept around the stone wall and found a tiny hole through which the voices could be heard. He put his eye to the hole and saw Wulfad and Rufin, the brothers of the stubborn Werburgh. The stone wall was in fact the back of a cave, and Werbode could see the two princes sat inside talking with a man who had a wooden cross hanging from his neck. Werbode had often wondered why the princes' hunting expeditions had not been so successful recently and now he had the answer. This must be where they came each day and, from what he could hear, the two of them had become Christians. They were receiving counsel from this shadowy holy man rather than remaining true to Thor, the god of their fathers. And Werbode knew now how he could get his revenge on that woman who had made him look foolish. He would show her that those who crossed him would feel the anger of the mighty warrior Thor.

Rushing back to the castle, Werbode demanded an audience with King Wulfhere. Before the King's court, he declared that his sons had betrayed him. They had become Christians and were in the discipleship of a holy man. With relish, Werbode told of all he had seen through the hole in the cave wall, confirming Wulfhere's suspicions about his boys supposed hunting trips. Fury rose up in the heart of the King. No one tricked him, not even his sons. With a face like thunder, his voice boomed out from the throne, ordering his warriors to arm themselves and ride with him like lightning. They would set out from the castle, find those insolent boys and cut them from their lives.

Werbode's eyes glistened with glee as he saw the shock on the faces of Werburgh and her controlling mother. He would return from this hunt with the King and then take a weakened Werburgh as his own. The princess, however, was not as enfeebled by this news as the arrogant warrior presumed. As the King and his warriors marched from the great hall, she sent her maid-servant out on the fastest horse to ride out before the vengeful throng and warn her brothers before they came to the castle.

It was as Wulfad and Rufin came out of the woods, with a hare or two tied to their saddles to act as evidence of their supposed hunt, that their sister's maidservant rode breathlessly up to them. In halting words, she quickly gave them the news, but before she had finished her sentence there was the sound of hooves thundering over the land and cries ringing out towards them. The two princes did not need to ask more of the servant. It was clear that their deception had been found out. Turning their horses about, the two of them galloped off back into the woods.

Wulfhere led his warriors into the trees. Werbode saw Werburgh's maidservant sheepishly watching the warriors pass by. He cursed her and decided that she too would be taught whom to obey upon his return. Oh, how he would enjoy meting out the King's punishment on these two princes. And, how he would relish returning to the castle and putting in their place those women who thought they could pull the strings of men.

Breaking out from the woodland, the princes continued their escape. But when they travelled not more than 3 miles, Wulfad's horse tragically slipped. To Rufin's despair, his brother and steed fell, the prince being trapped under the body of the horse. Rufin turned to assist his fallen elder, but Wulfad cried out that he should not.

'Stay on your horse!' he cried, 'One of us must live. Ride; ride away. Find freedom for the sake of our mother and sister!'

Rufin faltered. His heart could not leave his brother, but he loved his mother and Werburgh. Suddenly, the sound of riders was heard again, descending on the two with bloodthirsty cries and the flash of their swords. Rufin pulled on the reins, turned his horse again and shot away in the hope of keeping his own life a little longer.

'We will meet again, brother,' he called out, 'In the halls of Heaven, we will drink together!'

I need not tell you what happened to Wulfad at the hands of his father's men. Suffice it to say that the prince joined the ranks of the countless martyrs from those days. And the unholy break that the band of warriors took allowed Rufin to gain further distance from his foes. Whether from his tears or from this sudden exertion, he was as dry as stone. He therefore stopped at a small spring outside of the village of Burston where both he and his horse could drink. Kneeling down, Rufin plunged his hands into the cool clear water, cupping the drink to his mouth and washing his head and face. He breathed a sigh of relief and rested for a few short moments, until there was the sound of a twang behind him. A thud in his back juddered through his body and a pain pricked his heart. In this moment of solace, the warriors had caught up with their prey. A second arrow quickly joined the first and the prince fell forward – his lifeless body welcomed by the spring.

Werbode laughed as he saw Rufin's wet and dripping body brought back to join the remains of his brother. But he was silenced as Wulfhere called out to his band of men.

'See then, what happens to those who try to deceive me. I am not one to be tricked and trifled with. These sons of mine, my own flesh and blood, are now dead. Their deceit is ended. If I am this way with my own, how will I be with anyone who dares defy me, Wulfhere, King of Mercia and of Kent, the dreadful son of Thor!'

As the warriors turned their horses to leave in silence, Wulfhere looked at the uncovered bodies of his sons. Those boys he had taught to hunt and to fight, now lying so still. Never again would he see them ride out to hunt – whether real or contrived. Never again would they fight alongside him – whether faithful or faithless. Never again would their laughter echo with his about the great hall – whether in jest or in breaking an embarrassed silence … only silence now remained.

Word had quickly arrived at the castle with the first warriors' return. As Werbode rode up the hill beside his King, he was taken aback to see Ermenilda, Werburgh and their entourage riding out towards them.

'Why are you leaving?' he growled at the princess, 'Our King has destroyed those who are untrue. Now is the time to show your loyalty.'

'I go to bury the dead,' answered Werburgh, her eyes challenging the warrior's irritation, 'My dead brothers.'

'Your brothers defied …'

But he was cut off by the King.

'Enough!' barked the ruler, 'Leave them to their rituals and you return to your quarters at the castle.'

Werbode stared at the King, amazed, but knew that this was not an order to be questioned. He watched the princess's train continue on its mission, then turned back to follow the King, chastened and quietly seething.

The bodies of the slain princes were being overseen by those Christians who resided in the nearby villages and many had begun to cover them with stones, as was the custom of that time. Seeing the faces of her sons in that stone surround, Ermenilda uttered her farewells through a waterfall of tears, splashing onto the surface of those gathered rocks. Werburgh did the same, as the people continued to cover the bodies, and one man led the gathering in prayer. He stood in worn robes and around his neck there hung a wooden cross.

Back at Bury Bank, Wulfhere paced about the great hall alone. All had been banned. The King wanted no company.

His two sons were gone and this was by his own command. Until today, he had been so proud of his boys. And now he had driven a greater wedge between himself and those women he truly loved, Ermenilda and Werburgh. Anger burned like a forge in his heart as he strode back and forth across the rush-strewn floor. Not only anger at his sons, but anger at himself too. Was this the anger of Thor? But what good was the power of Thor if the lightning bolts of justice split not only rocks but families too!

Wulfhere flung back the doors of the hall and marched out to his horse. Riding hard, he set out for the ancient sacrificial stone, where he had honoured Thor so many countless times in blood. Here there was only rock – the hardness of stone. There was no room for sorrow in this place, no listening ear for grief. As Wulfhere cried out for Thor to hear him, the King's voice only echoed back, repeating his words of loss, reiterating his irreversible action. He needed forgiveness, but that could not be found here.

Wulfhere found himself wandering. How many hours he drifted, the King could not tell, but soon he was tracing a path unfamiliar to him. A path that had been taken many times by his sons. It was in this wooded spot that he lost all notice of his steps and slowed his pace, his feet padding on the pine-covered floor. He was now following only his heart and looking deeper into himself. But would he find something to bring him hope? Then a cry of 'Hold!' made his heart leap.

The King looked up to his left and there, standing in front of the entrance to a cave, was a man in long, worn robes. The stranger beckoned for Wulfhere to join him, and, after climbing up the small hill, Wulfhere met with the man, who furnished him with a humble but welcome offering of bread, fish and wine.

It was here that Wulfhere heard the story he had banned from his sons. It was the story of a father who had lost his son. It was one of grief and loss, but one which led to the hope of forgiveness. And it was there, surrounded by the hardness of stone, that Wulfhere, King of Mercia and Kent, found an open heart. Release came to the stricken man and he saw a way to begin again. Taking on the forgiveness offered by Christ, this man walked out from the cave to follow the path he had so cruelly stopped his sons from pursuing. This time, the father would follow in his sons' footsteps.

Reunited with his wife and daughter, Wulfhere became the first truly Christian King of Mercia. He allowed Ermenilda and Werburgh to build a church at the spot where his sons' bodies now lay, covered in stones. It was not long until a settlement built up around that church, and very soon it grew into the town we know today as Stone. The village of Burston still stands, with the tiny charming Church of St Rufin a stone's throw from the spring where the prince lost his life. And at Lichfield, St Chad's Well is still easily found, where the brothers were baptised and where, no doubt, the King also made his own declaration of faith.

St Werburgh's Story

I have already mentioned Werburgh and her resilience to the wiles of Werbode. I have told of her brothers' sad end and her father's repentance. So now it would be good to tell Werburgh's own story. It seems that, as a saint, Werburgh needed a story and, despite all her great work around Mercia, the holy woman was lacking a little in the line of miracles. Initially, tales were told of how she had corralled a flock of geese into a sheep pen and, despite the pen being open to the air, none of the geese had flown out. However, with other saints being known for healings and resurrections, this miracle seemed rather minor. The following addition to the original story was then told as the discovery of a forgotten detail, but I suspect it to be a fabrication, woven to give Werburgh's sainthood a little more clout.

Werburgh, as abbess, was concerned over how her holy sisters were constantly frustrated by some local geese. As the women attempted to sow the wheat and barley, the geese would come along and gobble up the grain before it had had a chance to root. Taking a shepherd's crook, Werburgh strode out into the fields in an attempt to round up the geese. Everyone thought that the woman would end up cheekily chasing the birds about, and that they'd simply fly up and over the would-be geese-herder. However, all were amazed to see that instead of flapping around Werburgh, the geese obeyed the woman's calls and cries. As she marched up to them, arms outstretched, with the crook in her right hand, the geese compliantly gathered together like a flock of feathered sheep, their only goose-like quality being their quiet honking. Then, Werburgh led the collected gaggle across the field to a nearby sheep pen. Holding the gate open with one hand, she guided her new flock in with the crook, shut the gate and made it secure – a tentative applause echoing over the fields from the abbey.

Now, I've already said how the geese remained in the pen, choosing not to fly out but waiting until Werburgh returned. The nuns continued with their sowing whilst their abbess spoke to the geese, gently berating them, saying that they must remain in the pen overnight as punishment for eating the grain. And that's where they remained.

However, early in the morning, whilst the abbess was leading
the sisters in prayer, one of the servants woke up looking for
some breakfast. He came out of his kitchens to make his way to
the stores, when he heard geese honking. He turned the corner
and saw, over by the fields, the geese that Werburgh had penned
in. He had not heard about the abbess's amazing actions the
day before, but simply saw that breakfast had been provided.
He chose a goose, killed it, plucked it and began to cook up a
delicious stew.

When Werburgh came out of morning prayers, she heard not
so much a honking coming from those geese in the pen, but more
of a squawking. Something was definitely wrong. She rushed out
of the abbey and across to the fields. Something had certainly
disturbed the geese, which still had not left their wooden cell, but
were flapping and hopping about in a most panicked manner.
Werburgh then noticed that not all of their number was present
– one was missing. She immediately suspected that someone
from the kitchens had taken one of the geese, and straight away
set off back to the abbey. Marching into the kitchens, she disturbed an embarrassed servant who was just about to enjoy a
goose meat stew. The abbess was furious and demanded that not
only he stop, but that he bring all the remains of the goose to her
now. Bones and feathers were then brought to Werburgh, who
placed them on the rough wooden table next to the bowl of stew.
Carefully, she arranged all the bones in an attempt to reconstruct
the skeleton. She then fished out the bits and pieces of good meat
from the stew and placed these with the assembled bones. And
finally she covered the goose remains with the feathers. Now she
needed to pray. Kneeling there in the kitchen, she commended
the sorry creature to God, reminding the Creator of how the
bird had obediently remained in the sheep pen and had been

slain through no fault of its own. And, as she fervently made her appeals, her eyes tightly closed, she heard, like a trumpet sound that morning, the excited honking of a goose. Opening her eyes, she saw not only the open mouth and staring eyes of the serv-- ant, but that goose alive and healthy striding up and down the kitchen table. She had to admit it had a bit of a limp, but it was certainly alive.

And so, with this miracle of reassembly and resurrection, Werburgh proved that she was worthy of the ranks of sainthood, and those Christians who venerated this abbess now felt justified.

The Founding of Stafford

Bert served Guthlac for many years and it seems that finally the Devil left him alone. Either that, or Bert had become better at resisting th'Olde Lad – still, 'resist the Devil and he will flee from you.' And so the relationship between Guthlac and Bert had moved onto better ground. That said, they still lived in that wet, boggy land of the Fens. It was through living in this place that Guthlac finally caught marsh fever, probably thanks to the mosquitos. His condition did not improve and, knowing he was going to die, Guthlac called his faithful friend to his bedside.

'Bert,' he whispered between the bouts of hot and cold, 'my dear faithful Berteline. When I pass on to be with our Father, take word to my sister. Do not stay here, but go find my dear Pega.'

Bert had never heard Guthlac speak of his sister. In fact, he had been noticeably quiet on anything to do with his family.

'Where will I find her?' Bert asked.

'She is at Peakirk,' Guthlac spluttered, as a bout of fever and shaking came on him again.

Bert soothed Guthlac's brow with a cool, damp cloth and assured him that he would head off to Peakirk forthwith.

But then the master grasped Bert's sleeve and pulled him in close.

'Wait!' his eyes implored this partner in Christ and in that moment his shaking stopped, his body was still. 'Tell her that I have in this life avoided her presence so that in eternity we may see one another in the presence of our Father, amid eternal joys. I have loved her always – loved her too much. But as I have given her up so we shall be rewarded with one another in Paradise.'

Then Guthlac slipped into oblivion, falling back onto his pillow and releasing Bert.

A little confused, but certain of his task, Bert packed his bags and loaded up a small boat to journey up the river to Peakirk. In taking this trip he was in fact retracing a trip Pega herself had taken many years ago when she and Guthlac had departed from one another's company. Pega had taken a small vessel to follow the course of the river until she came to an area of land which she felt was a lot drier than that of the Fens. It was here that she began her ministry and saw a church built. The place became known as Pega's Church and later Peakirk.

As Bert climbed out of the boat onto that firm, dry land, he wondered why Guthlac had never mentioned his sister when she lived so close and the place was even named after her. Still, he had a task to do for his mysterious master and so he went to the church to find Pega. It did not take him long as she was praying at the altar. She turned to Bert as he entered the cold stone building, but did not say a word. There were tears in her eyes and Bert guessed that she already knew. He told her all the same – that is why he had come – and his words affirmed what she had sensed in her soul. Still saying nothing, Guthlac's beloved sister arose and left the church to prepare for her journey to Crowland. And Bert was left alone in the still and silent place. His hand fumbled at the bag, which was on his shoulder. He had packed all his possessions and brought them with him. Why had he done that? As Bert saw the last rays of the sunset coming in through the church windows, he decided to spend that night in the church. It was no use leaving now, not when it was getting dark. So using his bag as a pillow, he settled down on the stone floor. It may have been cold and hard, but at least it was dry, and there were no mosquitos.

From Peakirk, Bert returned to his wanderings. With Guthlac's death he wasn't sure there was anything more for him in Crowland and so he continued in a westerly direction. After several days, he found himself at the banks of the River Sow and there, in the middle of the river, was a lonely island. Bert needed some time alone and perhaps this would be the place where he would find some space to reflect and pray, and decide where he should go next. Walking along that riverbank, he soon found a ferryman. As they made their way over to the island, the ferryman asked Bert where he had come from. It had been a while since Bert had spoken properly to anyone and before he knew it much of his life story tumbled out there in the boat. The ferryman was most fascinated with Berteline's tales of the Devil.

'Ooh, so we have a man here who has seen off th'Olde Lad!' he laughed with admiration. 'You must be a holy man then?'

Bert just shrugged. There was a time when he would have liked to have described himself in this way, but that was when he was younger and knew nothing of hardship.

'I reckon you are a holy man,' the ferryman continued. 'You have a Bible there under your robes. You've seen miracles. You are withdrawing to a lonely place to read Scriptures. Wait till my wife hears about this.'

Bert tried to dissuade the man from telling people. He had actually come to this island for some solace and to work out where his life should go next. It didn't take long however for the people to start arriving. They wanted to learn from Bert, to hear of his encounters with the Devil and to see if he had any other miracles up his sleeves. He was a kind man and he had learnt many things from his service under Guthlac, and so Bert taught the people, prayed for them and even witnessed some healings. Together they built a church there and Bert erected a large wooden cross. Some of those people became his followers and small dwellings were built on the island. The village on the riverbank, Bethney, began to grow as more came to see this holy man and join the faithful community. And Bert realised then that the place he should be next was right there on that island, with those people, fostering a new community here in Mercia.

As the years passed the people managed to ford the river, making it easier to reach Berteline's island, and the village grew bigger and bigger. The people still took boats back and forth from Bethney, but it had grown so much and become so busy that those who moved into the area referred to it as a quay or staithe. And it wasn't long until that staithe-ford town became known as Stafford.

Word of this incredible little town spread throughout the kingdom of Mercia and tales of a holy man behind it all were woven into these stories. Then the King of Mercia came to hear of all this and, on hearing such tales, he decided that he would like to see this place for himself, to meet this legendary holy man.

It was as Berteline was finishing the leading of morning Mass that he saw a crowd of men on horseback gathered at the staithe readying to ford the river. It was not usual for such men to attend Mass here at his holy island and besides, they were too late. But as the horses splashed through the water, making their way towards Berteline's residence, the holy man gasped. He immediately recognised the one who was leading this galloping troop. It was his father, the King of Mercia. Berteline quickly turned and ran to his cell. Slamming the door behind him, Bert fell to his knees in panic. Thoughts of those days when he had thrown away his princely status in the hopes of becoming a holy man raced through his mind. How he had run away to Ireland to follow in the footsteps of St Patrick. How he had returned to Mercia to discover that his father had banished him from the kingdom and if he was ever found to be in Mercia again he would be killed. That was years and years ago – surely his father would not be angry with him now. Bert stood up, remembering that he was now a true holy man. He had a community about him, which respected him. The town of Stafford had grown up thanks to the hope he had brought the people of Bethney. Surely his father would see all this and forgive the churlish behaviour of his youth.

The door to his cell suddenly flew open as if hit by a rush of wind. It swung back on its hinges to hit the stone wall behind and in strode the King – Berteline's father. Bert bowed respectfully to the man, a warrior king, who even in these later years maintained the stature of one who had clearly been victorious in countless battles, defending his land and people. The King sat on the one seat in the cell, but in the dim light of that tiny dwelling seemed not to recognise the man before him.

'So then, holy man,' boomed the voice of the King, 'What is your name?'

Instinctively, without thought, in answer to this simple question, that fear-ridden son began to say Berteline. But before he could utter the whole name he realised what he was about to say and so his hands leapt up to cover his mouth. What the King heard then was something more like 'Bertmm-mm-mm'.

'Bertmm-mm-mm?' asked the King. 'Bertmm-mm-mm? What kind of name is that?'

Bert said nothing.

'My ears must be losing their hearing in my old age. You must have said Bertram, did you not?'

'Yes, your Majesty,' lied the holy man. 'That is exactly it. My name is Bertram.'

And so Bert breathed a sigh of relief thinking he had managed to avoid a very tricky situation.

Bert then took the King about his holy island and back across the ford, so that he could see the whole town of Stafford. The King was impressed and gave his full permission and backing to

Bertram, allowing him to continue his ministry to the people of Bethney and Stafford.

When the King left, Bert needed to have a lie down. He had thought that at any moment his father would recognise his son and then there'd be Hell to pay. But he hadn't and now both Bert and his people had royal recognition. That was until the King died and a new ruler came to the throne …

THE CHALLENGE OF THE CHAMPIONS

Many years later, a new king came to the throne of Mercia. I am not sure as to how Bert's father died, nor why the holy man did not now make a claim to the throne himself. However, the new king was hostile to the religion of Christianity and had no desire to allow precious land to be taken up by churches and holy men. It was during this time that Bert saw that a king was again visiting his island. It was the new King of Mercia who was being brought across the River Sow by the local ferryman. The King stood up proud in the boat, eyeing this holy island with contempt, but being a holy man Bert came and welcomed this visitor with the hospitality he offered to all who came across the water. The King was not willing to sit and share food or drink with this Christian. He had come to issue Bert with an ultimatum.

'I am King of Mercia now and this land rightly belongs to me. I see you have quite a set-up here, with your church and cross and your own hovel, as well as a number of tumbledown houses for your followers. Well, I am not an unreasonable man. I will give you permission to remain here and practise your religion – who knows, you might get to be good at it and not need the practice!'

The King laughed at his own joke. Bert was relieved to hear that he and his followers could stay, and so he laughed along with the King, willing to forgive this slight dig.

'Yes,' continued the King, 'you can stay, but on one condition.'

Bert stopped laughing.

'Tomorrow morning, you must face my champion. My greatest warrior will arrive here at first light and you will face him in one-on-one combat. If you win the fray, then you will of course be allowed to remain on this island and promote whatever faith you so desire. But, if you should lose, and still live, then you will be banished from this island and from my kingdom forever more. Understand?'

The King could not have made it clearer, but Bert needed to confirm he had understood everything right.

'Your Majesty, am I right in thinking that I must face your greatest warrior, despite not being a man of war, but a man of prayer?'

'You are right indeed,' the King chuckled. 'However, if you can find any who will fight on your behalf, then I will allow them to be your champion. Know you of one who would volunteer?'

Bert wracked his brains thinking of all those who had visited the island and benefited from his ministry. They were generally farmers, not warriors. Some could be handy with a pitchfork and others would stand up to defend their own land. There may even be a fearsome blacksmith across the water in Stafford, but would anyone be willing to fight as his champion? In a battle that would likely lead to their death?

Bert sighed, looked at the grinning monarch and shrugged his shoulders.

'Ha, you have until tomorrow morning to find out,' laughed the unkindly King. Then turning about he marched back to the ferry, calling back, 'At first light, remember. My champion will be here at first light.'

As Bert watched the King sailing away he realised that he could not ask anyone to stand in his place. He had given hope to many of the people of Bethney, but they were not warriors. It was likely that the King's champion was the best in the land and to ask any of his people, men of the soil, to face the coming man-at-arms would be unkind and unreasonable. Bert turned to face his church and saw the old cross which he had set up in those early days when he had first begun preaching on the island. Without a second thought he walked over to that great holy symbol, knelt down before it and began to pray. Over and over he affirmed his weakness and his need for God to aid him. He prayed for his people and their future. If he, Bert, should lose this conflict then what would happen to those who had come to live on the island?

'Lord, send someone to my aid, send someone, please,' he prayed over and over, through the remainder of the day and into the night.

Word of the King's challenge very quickly spread through the island, across the water and to the town of Stafford, and an anxiety rattled through the hearts of the people. But when they saw their holy man, Bert, on his knees before the cross and saw that he was there hour after hour, a reassurance quelled the fears of many. Not all, however, as some felt that Bert's time would be better spent practising with a sword rather than clutching his hands and babbling to himself.

Night passed and in the cold of the early morning, Bert continued in his prayers. The first rays of sunlight would soon appear and with them would come the King's champion. In the silence of that misty morning, Bert's whispers fluttered about the island, until he heard a footstep behind him. Then he felt a bony finger tap him on the back. Stiff from the long hours on his knees in the damp air, Bert heaved himself about to see who it was that approached him from behind. And there in the half-light stood a tiny man.

'I am here in answer to your prayers,' piped up the little man, his voice breaking the morning like a blue tit.

Bert stared at the would-be warrior. 'You?' he said, as he saw the sword that this volunteer carried. It was closer to the size of a toothpick than a formidable weapon. 'Aren't you a little small to take on the King's champion?'

The little man rolled his eyes, 'And you are supposed to be a holy man! Have you not heard of the story of David and Goliath?'

Bert nodded.

'Well then,' the little man continued, 'if the shrimp beat the giant then, it could happen today also. I have been sent by God and if you are willing, I will be your champion.'

Bert felt chagrined to be reminded of Bible stories. After all, it was the public reading of the Scriptures that had first led him into the role of a holy man.

'I am sorry,' he said, slowly rising, his knees still very stiff. 'I will of course accept you as my champion. And it appears I have no choice…' For the sun's rays had now appeared over the horizon and he could hear the oars of the ferryman swishing through the waters. The King's champion was on his way.

On the bank of the island stood the King, together with his champion – a man of 7ft tall, encased in armour and carrying not only sword and shield, but spear and axe and a spiked ball on a chain. Meanwhile, Bert stood with his rough robe pulled tight around him in the chill of the morning, together with his champion – a man of barely 3ft tall brandishing only something that appeared to be best for skewering pickled onions. The King could not stifle his laughter. This duel was going to be even more

fun than he had first imagined. And a giggling sound was heard from deep within the thick beard of the armoured giant.

Then the sun, which was quickly rising in the sky, shone down with a strength that surprised them all that morning; it bathed the tiny warrior in its light. The laughter of the King and the champion soon faded as that little man glowed and before their eyes began to grow. His arms expanded to be bound in muscle, his clothing became shining armour, and that dainty weapon of a toothpick extended to become a chieftain's sword. And now standing before them all was the greatest warrior any had ever seen. His size dwarfed the King's own champion. His blade glistened in the sunlight, as did his armour and the shield which rested on his arm.

It did not take long for the King's champion to recover his wits from this sight. He had come to win this day and although this was an opponent he had not expected to fight, fight he must. With a roar, the champion raced forward swinging the spiked ball about his head. Bert's warrior stepped forward, with his sword ahead. The whizzing chain caught on the blade and in its momentum wrapped about the sharp weapon. Bert's warrior then flipped the sword back over his head to send the spiked ball flying behind him, way across the island, chain and all. The King's champion took up his axe and swung it at his enemy, who placed his shield in the way. Such a blade would have split any obstruction, but not this shield. Instead, the axe head slid off its shaft and fell off onto the ground. The King's champion then ran back to throw his spear at Bert's warrior, aiming for the eye-slits in his helmet. But the giant caught the projectile in his teeth – who had the toothpick now! – and spat it out into the river. So now it was to be a fight with sword and shield. The King's champion raced forward again with his weapons at the ready, but this final attack was short-lived too. Bert's warrior swung his shield to smash the King's champion in the chest, knocking him to the floor. Then reaching down that giant took up the man by the ankle. And now it was that man's turn to discover what it was like to be spun about the head. Swinging him about like a doll, the giant whizzed his opponent around and around until finally he let go and that poor warrior went flying through the air. He did not need to use the ferry to leave the island that day. He disappeared over a distant hill as his cries echoed out over the fields. And he was never seen again.

Then the warrior on the bank turned to the amazed holy man.

'Don't stand with your mouth open, Bert. You prayed for help and it has been granted you.'

Bert closed his mouth and rubbed his eyes, and saw standing before him was the little man who had first volunteered his services in the early hours of the morning.

'Thank you,' Bert whispered in disbelief.

'Don't thank me – thank God,' said the tiny warrior, who then leapt up into the air – a great leap which took him way above the heads of both the holy man and the King, into the clouds and presumably back to Heaven.

Bert then turned to the King, but saw he was heading back to the ferryman in quite a hurry.

'Your Majesty?' called Bert, chasing after the fast disappearing crowned head.

'The land is yours,' called back the King. 'Stay on this island as long as you wish. Worship whoever you like.'

Almost slipping down the riverbank, the frightened King leapt into the boat, ordering the ferryman to get him back to shore as quickly as possible.

Having gained royal permission to stay, and with divine aid too, the faith of the people of Stafford was greatly increased. For Bert, however, things never felt quite the same. He was getting old now and he could not keep up with all the needs of these people. He was pleased that a Christian presence could remain in this part of Mercia, but he began to believe it was time for him to leave. Bert looked at how his people were caring for one another, teaching each other, and how there was true life in the town. He could leave them now, he thought. They would survive without him, maybe even thrive. So he quietly left, taking his own boat across the river one night, and began to retrace those steps he had taken so many years ago.

ST BERTRAM'S WELL

Leaving the people of Stafford to finally find a quiet place to be with his own thoughts and prayers, the elderly Bertram, as he was now known, walked north-east and found himself on the far edges of his father's kingdom again. He was in the Peak District once more. It must have been late morning, say 11 a.m., that he arrived in a region he recognised and felt comforted by this softer side of the Moorlands. It was many, many years ago that he had been in these parts, but for far unhappier reasons. Near here, outside of Wetton, Bert and his princess bride from Ireland had sheltered in a cave. They had been on the run from Bert's father, but his wife had been with child. She had therefore sheltered in Thor's Cave whilst he went over the hills to find help. He was still haunted at darker moments by the sound of those wolves – the wolves which had been living in that cave and had ravaged both his wife and the unborn child. But that had been so long ago, and much had happened since. Now Bert was in the twilight of his life, he would again like to be up there, close to where he had lost his beloved.

It was there then, outside of Ilam, that he made his home by a natural spring and would sit under a tree contemplating the Scriptures and all he had seen happen in his long years. That was until word spread again that there was a holy man in the area. The people of Stafford had also been shocked to discover that their holy man was no longer with them. A search was made and word went out. Some of the people of Ilam had noticed a hermit-like figure wandering about the Bunster hills and information had been exchanged between them and the people of Stafford. And so again, Bert found he was receiving visitors looking for spiritual guidance. He would welcome them and give them water from the spring. If any had received cuts and bruises in their efforts to find him, Bert felt compelled to use the leaves of the tree to soothe their wounds. And again, the people were healed. This of course meant that the word spread with greater power and soon Bert was hosting a centre of pilgrimage up there in the hills of the Staffordshire Moorlands. His spring became known as St Bertram's Well and the tree, watered by the healing waters under the earth, continued to produce healing leaves, making whole more than just those who had cuts and bruises.

This place of pilgrimage could not have been more different from that of Guthlac's where Bert had received his training. Here now he was close to his wife, the ground was hard and dry, the water was pure and he sat under a tree of healing. Although he was not able to really retire, Bertram thought that things could have been a lot worse. It seemed he was destined to care for others and bring them hope. If he could do this, remain dry and avoid marsh fever, then all the better.

And so it was that this saint of Mercia finally came to the end of his days on the earth. No martyrdom brought his life to an abrupt end. This runaway prince of Mercia had travelled many miles, learnt many lessons – including those of love and loss, had resisted the Devil, seen a town grow up around him, witnessed bizarre and fantastic miracles, and had simply been human throughout it all. He stretched out to sleep in his little cell up there at Bunster one more time. And as he rested, he heard footsteps outside. Was this another pilgrim? One coming so late. He sat up and looked out the window, ready to rise up and serve again. However, in the moonlight he saw the silhouette of a woman, a young woman who stood hand in hand with a child. They appeared to have passed Bert's cell and were walking slowly away. Bert knew who they were immediately and he leapt out of his bed. With a vigour he had long forgotten, he rushed to the door and without a thought was out under the moonlight. Leaving his body behind, his soul chased after the woman and child as they sauntered away up over the hills. And so Bert's long years on the earth had come to their end.

The people of Ilam discovered the body of the holy man who had adopted their home as his own. His body was therefore entombed there in that village at the Church of the Cross, where now there is a shrine to St Berteline. However, so well loved by the people of Stafford was their Bertram, that soon a request was made by the people that they should have their holy man back with them. The body was taken back to the town which Bertram had founded. And if you should visit that county town, you are still able to see the sight where Bert had his church. In the grounds of St Mary's Church, the outline of St Bert's chapel is shown, and in the middle lies a large, worn piece of wood, the remains of the cross which Bert set up to preach from and where he knelt in prayer for a champion.

ETHELFLEDA OF TAMWORTH

Some call her Æthelflaed, which is probably more accurate, but I prefer the name Ethelfleda. She was the warrior daughter of Alfred the Great and sadly a woman from British history of whom very few people seem to have heard. However, as Lady of the Mercians and effectively Queen of Mercia she has some great stories and had quite an influence on Staffordshire.

By the time she was married to her father's friend, Ethelred, Ethelfleda had already shown herself to be a great warrior and proved that her father was right in not sending her to a convent

– her mother's preferred option. Together then, Ethelfleda and Ethelred protected the kingdom of Mercia from the marauding Danes and the Norsemen coming in from the Irish Sea. Of course, Ethelred being older meant that soon he could not partake in many of the decisions necessary for running a small kingdom and so his lady took over defending England in the west whilst her brother, Edward the Elder, ruled Wessex and did his best to keep the Danes at bay.

Together Wessex and Mercia stood their ground at Tettenhall, where there was much rejoicing on the death of three enemy kings. But soon after this victory, Ethelred died. It was normal in such circumstances for the wife of such a nobleman to retire to a nunnery and a new ruler to be selected. However, Ethelfleda had earlier shown that embroidery and prayers were not for her. She, like Boudicca before her, would remain ruler despite the death of her husband.

It was then that she began to put her energies into strategically defending her people. There had been some trouble with the Norsemen up at Chester, which she put right using the bees of that city, but she knew these Vikings could be tricky. It was only a matter of time before they tried it again. She therefore began a burh-building project right across her land. Starting at the River Mersey, she built a string of fortresses, which would stand as strongholds against the Danes and Norsemen and so increase the protection of Mercia. From Runcorn, the line of burhs included Eddisbury, Bridgnorth, Chirbury and Warwick, as well as Stafford and Tamworth. It was at Stafford that she came across the cult of St Bertram. She was intrigued by the following this rather peculiar saint had and so introduced him to the most northerly part of her kingdom, building a chapel in his name (as St Berteline) which looked out across the

River Mersey. However, it was at Tamworth that she made her base of operations. From here she rode out, again to join forces with her brother. On to Derby Ethelfleda and Edward went and freed the city from the Danelaw. Spurred on by this victory, they turned their attention to Leicester and did the same there, so bringing the two cities under Anglo-Saxon rule again.

The son and daughter of Alfred the Great were a formidable team. They had trained together when young and now fought side by side, to maintain their father's vision to have a truly Anglo-Saxon Britain. Ethelfleda then took very much to Edward's son, Athelstan. He was the son she wished she could have had. She did have a daughter, Elfwyn, and Ethelfleda had tried to teach her the ways of battle which had come so naturally to the Queen when she was a girl. Elfwyn did try to swing the sword and thrust the blade as her mother had shown her, but it wasn't really her thing. She preferred sewing and really loved what you could do with a few coloured threads and a needle. In the evenings she would show her mother the embroidery she had been work-ing on between sword-practice and Ethelfleda would smile, but both could tell they were looking for something different in life. However, when Ethelfleda was with Athelstan, it was like he was her own child. He relished the fighting skills she taught him and then he would practise with his father when she had gone home. How she looked forward to seeing the boy again and noting how he had developed. And then she would sigh, thinking of her own child.

As the years went on, the Lady of the Mercians wondered what state her kingdom would be in when she had passed away and left it to Elfwyn. The Danes would certainly begin attack-ing Mercia again once she had gone, but she just couldn't see Elfwyn standing up to them. Danes had as much appreciation for embroidery as Ethelfleda. And so she had a quiet word with her brother. Something she did not tell her daughter about, but which would be best for her people.

Again, Ethelfleda and Edward were off defending Britain. This time it was York where they forced the Vikings to surrender. Enthused by this victory, Ethelfleda turned to head back to Mercia only to hear that in her absence the Danes had attacked Tamworth. It was starting already. Riding full speed, Ethelfleda summoned more of her troops and descended on Tamworth. How dare the Danes take her city! With her faithful people within the city walls and loyal soldiers fighting alongside her outside, they managed to take Tamworth back for Saxon England and so rebuilt the defences.

Ethelfleda then marched furiously over to see her daughter, Elfwyn, who was working on a beautiful tapestry depicting the battle. Ethelfleda sighed, she had sadly been right in what she had arranged with her brother.

Very soon after this event, Ethelfleda died. We are not sure what killed her, but people died younger in those days and she had done a lot of riding and killing in the past few days. Perhaps her body could take no more. It was after the funeral that Edward the Elder requested a meeting with his niece, Elfwyn. She welcomed him and showed him how well she was doing now with wielding a sword, just like her mother, but she also had some clever cross-stitching to share with him. Edward sat down and took a deep breath, then very kindly noted how Elfwyn so enjoyed needlework and how she perhaps had a gift. He went on to ask her how she would like to do that kind of thing every day, and so not worry about swords and fighting any more. Elfwyn's eyes lit up and Edward knew that his sister had been right. Elfwyn was then welcomed into the sisterhood of an abbey in Wessex where she was very happy and Edward was happier still. He was now King of both Wessex and Mercia, and although he missed his sister, he liked what she had left him.

At Tamworth Castle, the site of Ethelfleda's burh, there stands a statue showing the warrior queen, Lady of the Mercians, together with a child. She has her sword drawn and appears to be teaching the child. It is not her daughter, Elfwyn, but is in fact her nephew, Athelstan. And this is how Ethelfleda is remembered.

THE TAMWORTH LEGEND

This story is set soon after the Norman Conquest, when the kingdom of Mercia had long been absorbed into a united England, but I include it here to close this section. Not only does it takes its name from Ethelfleda's city, but it also refers to St Modwen who began this section and so could be seen to provide a fitting end. However, if the story is to be believed on every point, then Modwen would have to have lived for over 200 years.

Let us begin then with Lord Marmion of Tamworth Castle. Lord Marmion was one of the knights who fought alongside William the Conqueror at the Battle of Hastings and so was rewarded with land and title as the Norman king took over the rule of England. To Marmion he gave Tamworth and much of the land surrounding it. Lord Marmion then began to make himself at home and use the land as he wished, which included seizing a nunnery dedicated to St Editha.

One night, Marmion was enjoying a deep sleep after a day's hunting. However, his sleep was soon disturbed when he felt a prodding in his side. He turned over in his bed, but still he was being prodded and poked. Annoyed, and in some pain, he sat up and shouted, 'Who is that? Who is there in the dark prodding me?'

He then gasped as he saw the answer to his question. In the darkness, there glowed a woman in white who was floating above his bed. He of course thought it was a ghost and started calling on all the saints he could think of to protect him. The woman shook her head and poked him again. This shut up the knight and the glowing woman then spoke.

'It's no use you calling all those saints, Marmion. I am not a ghost.'

'Then who are you?' demanded the knight, still a little shaken and rubbing his side.

'I am St Editha.'

Lord Marmion had to think. Out of all the saints he had just called on there had not been a St Editha. In fact, he wasn't sure he'd ever heard of St Editha.

St Editha sighed and shook her head, 'I am the woman who began the nunnery you have just taken for yourself.'

'Oh,' Marmion could see where this was going, but he wanted that nunnery and the land was his. 'Well, don't think I'm going to give it back.'

'Remember who has a stick,' she warned. 'But let me tell you my story and then you will know what sadness it is that you are causing.'

Then the saint lowered herself from floating above the knight and came to sit at the foot of his bed, stick still in hand.

'My father, Athelstan … son of Edward the Elder?'

Marmion shrugged. It seemed that this Norman didn't know much. Editha continued.

'My father wished to have me married to Sihtrigg as a way of appeasing the Norsemen. He said his father and aunty would have turned in their graves, but it was the only way he could see that would keep the peace here in the kingdom of Mercia.'

Marmion raised his eyebrows. He still wasn't sure what this woman was on about. Editha chose to ignore him.

'Well, I said I would only marry the Norseman if he was a Christian and Sihtrigg said he was. The marriage ceremony took place, but then, before the wedding night, he told me that he was not a Christian. I told him that there would be no consummation then. He told me that if there was no consummation then there would be no marriage. I told him that was fine. And he stormed off. The church annulled our marriage and my father's plan came to nothing.'

'Is this meant to be the sad bit?' yawned Marmion.

'Wait and listen,' snapped Editha. 'Well, then I was able to tell my father that I had never really wanted to get married. I wanted to attend a nunnery and devote my life to prayer and service. He said I got that from my Aunty Elfwyn, but he had seen that she was happy and perhaps I would be happy there too. He decided then to invite an old friend of his over to Mercia to talk to her about setting up an abbey nearby. Her name was Modwen and she had cured my brother of leprosy. My father said that he had meant to thank her properly for this and setting up an abbey in her name would be a good way to do it. Modwen came with two other holy women, Lynne and Osyth, and in consultation with my father a small place of prayer was set up at Polesworth.'

'Where the nunnery is,' interjected Marmion. He could definitely see where this was going now.

'Yes,' affirmed Editha. 'And I joined with the holy ladies to begin my service to God. Years later I became Abbess of Polesworth and then, about 100 years before you appeared on the scene, I died.'

'Sorry to hear it,' said Marmion, not disingenuously.

Editha sighed. 'I am a saint,' she said.

'Congratulations?'

'Now listen, Marmion,' Editha sat forward now. 'Tamworth suffered a lot of damage under the Danes not so long ago and when Edgar rebuilt everything he made me patron of the church here. The one practically at the foot of your castle. Those poor nuns up at Polesworth Abbey have been through a lot, helping all the folk here in Tamworth. There were a lot of pieces to pick up and although their service has been in honour of God, I don't want them losing heart.'

Lord Marmion shrugged. He wasn't really moved.

'Listen, Marmion. Those nuns have been on their knees day and night calling out to me, their founder, to help them. And here I am.'

Now Marmion listened. He was quite impressed that his action had caused a saint to step out of Heaven. But then he considered what St Editha was asking. There was a lot of land associated with that nunnery and couldn't they stay somewhere else? The church, perhaps. He said as much to the saint at the end of the bed.

'No, they cannot,' blustered Editha and she stood up. 'Polesworth Abbey is my abbey. My father set it up for me. It has been a source of comfort to the people of Tamworth for over 100 years. Give it back to the Church and stop being greedy!'

Marmion could see she was cross, but he failed to see why it was so important.

'Listen, Marmion,' said Editha, now lowering her voice and gritting her teeth. 'You have already tasted a good few prods from my stick. Are you really telling me that you would like that every night?'

Marmion rubbed his side again. He even moved back his night robe to take a look. It was bruised and that was just from one night.

'You'd really come back every night and prod me?'

'All through the night,' she said.

'It means that much to you?'

'Anything for my girls!' And she stared hard at Marmion.

The knight had to look away, but then he made a decision.

'Very well,' he said. 'Have it your way. I'll give the place back to the Church, just promise me that this is the last I see, or feel, of you.'

'You'll never know I exist.'

I didn't anyway, thought Marmion, who yawned and tried to get back to sleep.

The next morning, Marmion got himself ready and rode down to the church, St Editha's Church. He needn't have taken a horse. He could have walked. But being on horseback looked more impressive. And there he announced that he would like to give the nunnery back to the Church. The sisters who were there that morning were delighted and thanked Lord Marmion intensely. 'Oh, thank you Lord Marmion,' they cried. 'God bless you. This is wonderful news.'

Marmion turned the horse about.

'We will commend your soul to St Editha in our prayers every morning,' continued the nuns, calling out to him.

Marmion looked back. 'You will?' he asked.

The nuns nodded enthusiastically.

'Tell her I say hello,' he said and then rode back up to Tamworth Castle – rubbing his side.

4

Tales from
the Middle

I call this section 'Tales from the Middle' to distinguish the stories from those of the Moorlands in the north and the Black Country in the south. However, some of the tales contained here do come from areas which are distinctly part of the north or south of the county; areas which may not normally be considered to be in the 'middle'. I have put them here because they are not part of those two quite opposite regions of Staffordshire. The influence of the Mercian kings, queens and saints is felt in the 'middle'. They were responsible for the establishment of towns and cities, and are remembered in the place names. And the remains of their fortresses are often seen looking down from the hills on many a Staffordshire horizon, as a constant reminder of those days.

However, in later times it was the likes of Wedgwood, Cliff, and Rhead which not only provided jobs, but influenced changes on the landscape and the ordering of communities. This is especially true for the likes of Stoke-on-Trent, Tunstall and Burlsem, and there are a handful of stories here which grew out of this time. Eccentric characters began to appear and were talked about by those people living and working so closely together. Very soon they took on mythic proportions as tales of their exploits were handed down from one generation to the next. However, there are many towns and villages in Staffordshire that had little, if anything, to do with pottery and I have, of course, included tales from these too. A number are twists on distinctive points in history, localising great events, while others come from a relationship with the local landscape and some of its key features.

THE BLACK MEN OF BIDDLE

The people of Biddulph Moor have always been known for being different. In the past, many were described as being dark-skinned and there is even mention of distinctive red hair. The name Bailey is fairly prevalent amongst the people there, and various explanations have been given for all these features.

I have heard it said that during the Roman occupation, soldiers were brought over from Spain to work on Hadrian's Wall. On their return, they got lost and wandered throughout Britain until they finally decided to cut their losses and settle in the place we now know as Biddulph Moor, the people there now being descendants of this lost building crew.

But those who have studied the heritage of this unique area mention that in the early twentieth century the residents would greet one another by raising their hand and saying 'Saladin'. Is this more of a clue to their origins?

In the fifteenth century, Lord Orm of Knypersley returned to England from his campaign in the Crusades. The people of

Staffordshire were surprised and intrigued to see that he had brought with him a band of Saracens. These were not necessarily warriors – although some of them could certainly fight – they were actually master stonemasons. Many people from that region of the world had a high reputation for their stonework and Lord Orm, the Dragon Lord, thought that such people would be useful. He had it in mind to build a church at nearby Stafford, one that would be dedicated to St Chad. And so these Muslim crafts-men began work on this Christian place of worship. It was not unusual for such things to happen across Christendom in those days. What room for argument did those Saracens have anyway? Much like the Moors put to work on the chapels in southern Spain, Orm's Saracens set to climbing up and down ladders, and chipping away to create a unique church in Staffordshire.

Lord Orm ensured that these stonemasons were given resi-dence on Biddulph Moor in the shape of a temporary camp. From up there on the hills, the Saracens were able to look down on the peculiar dwellings of the local people huddled together in this unfamiliar damp climate. They were surrounded by red earth and a patchwork of lush green fields. It was certainly an alien landscape for these men.

Now, one of the Saracens who had returned with Lord Orm could speak perfect English. His name has been forgot-ten – in some ways – but he was known locally as the Paynim, a word similar to pagan, although he surely did not see him-self in this light. He was the leader amongst this band of Saracens, not only by virtue of his command of the English language, but also due to his education and status. In fact, during the long journey from the Holy Land across Europe, the English Channel and up through Britain, a friendship had developed between Lord Orm and this man. The Dragon

Lord had therefore decided not only to put the Paynim in charge of the Saracen band, but also gave him authority over the region in which Biddulph Moor was placed. He was to be Lord Orm's bailiff.

And so the stonemasons began work on St Chad's Church, regularly taking the journey down from Biddulph Moor to Stafford and often staying over in the town to continue their work. Of course, they would demand five breaks each day so that they might pray, but all wondered at their diligence and skill, as well as their designs.

When finished, the church certainly seemed to be a grand affair, standing not more than 250m from where St Bertram's first church lay. Yet it did look like a building plucked out of Palestine to be placed in the middle of England. Its box-like shape, with a gabled front end, offset by an imposing stone archway, was like nothing else in the region. However, it was the heads carved into the arch which drew the most interest. There was a series of unusually angular beasts surrounding the entrance, which looked down on all who entered. In the brickwork there was a number of geometric patterns, typical of Islamic stonework. But you could also see the occasional sheep's head – a reference to the shepherds of Palestine perhaps? And a moustached man's face – was this Lord Orm? But the most intriguing designs were on the pillars. Here there seemed to be lions or dogs; the people of Stafford were not sure which. But the Saracens knew. These were images of the Simurg, which they had adapted to look like dogs. The Simurg was a fabulous creature, part lion and part phoenix, and said to symbolise the wisdom of God. To their minds, this was a suitable image for such a place of worship. However, not wishing to create too much consternation, they had disguised their mythical beast.

To many it looked to be a dog, typical of many medieval churches. And where the Simurg's wings would normally be shown, raised and outspread, the masons had cleverly hewn what appeared to simply be a design based on the stem of a twisting plant. Those Saracens were clever. They took a pride in their work and their culture, but made sure that it was not too obvious. It was their secret.

Some of the masons worked on the font as well. A large stone structure which they again decorated with images they would not be unhappy with. With monkeys at its feet, lions surrounding its middle and four great pomegranates opening up to make the bowl, it was certainly not like any other font known to Lord Orm of Knypersley. It was too late when he noticed the female shapes worked in between the pomegranates, and how they appeared to be baring their breasts. Maybe these Saracens were not as devout as they had first made out.

Throughout this time, the Saracen bailiff continued to over-see the stonemasons, the camp at Biddulph Moor and many of the smaller surrounding villages. He was a thorough man who took an interest in the area and its people. He kept comprehensive records and was known for his fairness and diligence in all matters. It was not long then until Lord Orm introduced him to another of his bailiffs, one who had a daughter. Soon a marriage was arranged and the Paynim bailiff's suspicions were confirmed: his days would end in Staffordshire, but he was not unhappy. It was cold and damp here, but he enjoyed his tasks and he had earned the respect of the local people. And now he had a wife who soon gave him a child. As a fully integrated member of society, the bailiff chose to name his son in honour of the King. After all, if it wasn't for the King, he would not have been brought to England. So he named his son Richard. In fact, many of the Saracen stonemasons had found wives and their community grew. They soon became a distinct group of people, living up on Biddulph Moor, and they were recognised for their unique nature for many years and centuries thereafter. Throughout it all, they honoured both King Richard and Saladin.

If you should venture up to Biddulph Moor, take a look in the graveyard for the descendants of that Saracen bailiff, who became known as the Bailey family. You will be surprised to see how many Richard Baileys there are resting there. The name remained popular in the family even into more recent centuries.

Mow Cop

Mow Cop rises up on the landscape like a giant, the castle on its summit adding to its height like a royal crown. The arches, which almost frame the sky, certainly spark the imagination. In fact, there are many whispers associated with this hill, but few to do with those supposedly ruined remains. The castle is in fact a folly commissioned by Randle Wilbraham of Rode Hall. His hope was to set up a crumbling fortress which would provide a romantic picnic spot for family and friends. But some say that the wide arch is actually Spanish in origin, thanks to the residents of Biddulph Moor. As well as the story of Saracens coming to Biddulph Moor, others suggest that the first residents of this obscure village were in fact from Spain – either Iberian Romans or survivors of the Spanish Armada. There are many tales about the wealth of ships from the Armada getting lost in both the Irish Sea and the North Sea, with wreckages on the British coasts. Of course, those who survived had to make their way with care through the English countryside, often travelling at night for fear of being beaten and killed. But a small band found their way to this remote part of Staffordshire and decided to make a new home for themselves at Biddulph Moor. Their influence was felt all around, but is most clearly seen, some say, in the 'Spanish Arch' of Mow Cop Castle, their descendants being employed by Wilbraham for his extravagant building project.

Before all this, however, the Old Man of Mow probably stood alone on that hill, looking down to spy both across the Cheshire Plain and out to the Staffordshire Moorlands. This angular crop of stone sits in a lonely position on the cop and is said to have once been a cairn. However, it became the shape it is today through the quarrying that took place on the hill for many years. Alan Garner's book *Red Shift* describes a people who may have lived and worked on this site, but does not describe much in the way of happy experiences. In fact, there has often been talk of curses hanging onto the rocks here. This is all part of Mow Cop's mysteries, many of which still seem to be held tight behind its rocky face.

But in 1807, Mow Cop became the site which saw a new religious movement born. Inspired by the work of John Wesley, two local preachers, Hugh Bourne and William Clowes, called together a camp meeting to see the beginning of what would become known as Primitive Methodism. The day began with clouds hanging low over the hill, as if the curses of that place were rising up to intimidate the joyful throng. However, as people travelled in from the likes of Macclesfield and even from as far as Warrington, the clouds broke up and the sun shone down, heightening the anticipation of that excited gathering. Mind you, the weather did have plenty of time to clear up. That first meeting lasted fourteen hours!

And so Mow Cop holds three memorials to three differ-ent times. There is the Old Man of Mow, Wilbraham's Castle and an engraved plaque commemorating the founding of the Primitive Methodists. Three quite different features, represent-ing the three faces of this ancient hill.

THE WITCH OF BURSLEM

There was an old woman in Burslem whom everyone knew was a witch but nobody had much proof, until she died. Her name was Molly Leigh and she would sell milk, carrying a pail upon her head. Wherever she went, a raven would always accompany her. The bird would fly about from tree to tree as Molly went on her deliveries, and when she set down the bucket, the raven would come wheeling down out of the tree and rest upon her shoulder. It seemed that this black bird was her only friend and many thought that it was her witch's familiar. At times, the raven would caw loudly and even though people knew then that Molly was about with the milk, there were some who found it a great annoyance. One was the local parson, who one day was attempting to enjoy a pint of ale at the local pub. He heard the constant crowing outside and it wound him up so much that he grabbed a gun from the landlord, went out and shot at the bird which was perched up on the inn's swinging sign. The parson was not a bad shot and he hit the bird in the chest. But despite this, the raven fluttered up into the air and flew off unscathed, except for maybe losing one or two feathers.

A few days later, the parson began to complain of chest pains and when he told people about his attempts to shoot Molly's raven, they put two and two together. Of course, she was a witch. The parson had attempted to harm her familiar and now he was the one feeling like he had been shot in the chest. But all this was simply gossip and imagination. Very soon they would have something more solid to base their conclusions on.

It happened on the day Molly Leigh died. Many wondered who would now deliver the milk, but soon the cawing of the raven was heard again. Many said that the bird did not know where to go or what to do now that Molly had passed on. Some looked out to see what the raven was up to and they got a shock, for there was Molly. She was again wandering the streets with a pail of milk on her head, the raven fluttering from tree to tree. And as she did so her voice was heard repeating words the people of Burslem had not heard before:

Weight and measure sold I never,
Milk and water sold I ever.

This continued until she reached the end of the street, whereupon she disappeared, only to appear again on another night repeating the same ritual. These appearances caused much upset in the community, but there was worse to come. A number of people reported that Molly had suddenly appeared in their own homes. They would hear the caw of the raven and turn to see Molly sat in the corner of the room knitting away as if she was in her own home. And from her lips there tumbled a constant stream of mutterings, spells and incantations, being spoken as her knitting needles clicked away. Then another caw and she would vanish.

With these strange goings-on, a flood of people descended on the parson, demanding that he do something to ensure Molly's soul had been laid properly to rest. The parson could see the upset, but was worried about taking on a witch's spirit. He had been spooked by the chest pains following his previous encounter with the raven. He therefore called in a number of other clergy to help him.

The holy band of men set up a pig's trough in the church – something to catch the spirit in. And then the seven of them began to pray that Molly Leigh's spirit would find rest. As they prayed and recited passages from the Bible, a chill was felt through the church and Molly appeared, floating above them. With renewed fervour, the clergy prayed and slowly the witch's spirit came down from the roof and into the pig's trough. Then, quickly, the men picked up the trough and carried it out of the church and into the graveyard. Flipping it over they emptied the spirit onto Molly's grave, but still they could hear her voice:

> Weight and measure sold I never,
> Milk and water sold I ever.

The parson and his colleagues were at a loss as to what to do next, until one noticed something at the foot of a nearby tree. It was a black bundle of feathers, Molly's old raven, but now dead.

'We must bury it with the woman,' said the parson.

One of the men ran to fetch a spade and then he dug into the grave, Molly's voice slowly becoming more faint. The raven was then placed under the earth together with its old mistress and, when the two were completely covered, Molly's voice was heard no more.

Neither Molly nor her raven were seen again after that, and the whole of Burslem breathed a sigh of relief. But who was going to deliver the milk now? Maybe they could contact another Molly …

MOLLY ALBIN OF HANLEY

The idea of a female town crier may sound to be a modern concept, what with opportunities for women opening up throughout the twentieth century. However, it was about 200 years ago when a woman did fulfil this role. It was in Stoke-on-Trent, and there they all knew of a woman by the name of Molly Albin of Hanley, who certainly made the post of town crier her very own.

❧

Molly Albin was painfully aware of how she had taken on a role most commonly associated with men, but she could bellow with the best of them and stood with such self-assurance that very few wanted to challenge her. Besides, many recognised the value of having a town crier in Hanley and welcomed Molly's clanging bell in the hope of hearing the news she bore.

Molly divided her time between being a town crier and a seller of milk. She was not a milkmaid, but a woman of enterprise, being effectively a one-person dairy company. She would buy milk from the local farms and then start her rounds, delivering to the people of Hanley – home to those workers of the potteries. This brought in some money, but for Molly the crying out of the daily news added a little more to her income. In fact, it soon proved to be quite a lucrative business.

As town crier, Molly realised that her bell and her bellow would gain the attention of all who happened to be in the vicinity. She had also noticed that many of the men of Hanley seemed to be taking liberties. Not only taking liberties with their wives and families, but also with their employers. Having got to know many people through her deliveries, she was pretty much aware of where each man worked and what his household was like. She was, however, shocked to discover that some of them preferred to prop up the bar of the local pub rather than take their earnings back to their wives. Molly then saw the opportunity she had been given – recognised her calling, if you like. She may have been known for bringing the news of the day to the streets, but now she would bring some news that no one had expected to hear.

'Hear ye! Hear ye! Hear ye!' she cried, with her clamorous bell ringing out across the cobbled streets. 'Know then that Joseph Bourne is drinking himself into a stupor there in the pub across the way. Who would believe that such a man had a wife and five children waiting for him at home, needing him to bring back his earnings so that they might be fed! Shame on Joseph Bourne!'

Many who heard this were shocked. Some because of Joseph's actions, but others because they were worried that Molly would reveal their whereabouts when they had decided to take a drink or five before heading home after work. In Joseph's case, his wife heard the 'news' and stormed over to the pub together with the children. She was under the impression that her husband had been taking on extra work, but here he was drinking away their money. All then laughed to see him dragged out by one ear, his wife screaming in the other and a line of bewildered children following on.

With such success, Molly Albin decided to always keep an eye out. Once she had delivered the official news, she would do a circuit of the pubs looking to see who was there. Many who saw her arrive would suddenly drink up and head off home before they found their misdemeanours announced to all the world. Whilst others would hang on, even follow Molly about. They were looking forward to hearing what Molly would discover next. They could then laugh at the shamed husband, or maybe a worker who had given an excuse to his boss that he was sick or on family business. Molly would root them all out, layabouts and double-crossers. Anyone that Molly deemed not to be taking their responsibilities or commitments seriously. Whoever they were, Molly would expose them, proclaiming their whereabouts and their activities.

A number of employers therefore saw Molly as a great deterrent to any shirking that their workers might be considering. She was also helpful in finding those work-shy employees who had failed to turn up on any given day. So, Molly started to add to her earnings by being employed by the managers of the potteries; she made announcements in the streets about those who had failed to arrive at work. She would give a detailed and often colourful description of the offender and then encouraged all who heard it to send the lazy oaf to work if they should see him. Many would gather to hear Molly's pronouncements, enjoying the game of guessing who she was talking about and then laughing when they had worked it out; chuckling over how she had exaggerated certain aspects of their look and character.

This kind of work soon brought Molly a number of enemies. Those who had taken to avoiding work did not thank Molly for making the matter public and many threatened her with violence. But Molly was not one to be put off by these non-exposed louts. 'How dare they think they can get away with diddling their bosses, keeping money from their families or even beating their wives,' she thought. And besides, as well as her loud voice, Molly always carried with her that heavy bell. Anyone thinking they would mete out a beating on her would find her shout for help resounding over several streets. And a hefty bell can be brought swiftly to the head of any assailant – not something from which you would easily recover.

Yet, Molly was not as principled as you may think. Some of the cleverer employees saw that they too could make good use of the town crier and Molly always needed a little more money.

One evening, Molly appeared with her bell, giving the news as usual. 'Hear ye! Hear ye! Hear ye!' But once she had regaled the gathered crowd with the day's events, she did not do her usual rounds of the pubs; instead, she was joined by a strange-looking chap who appeared somewhat familiar to many of the working men gathered about.

'And hear now, all ye who are gathered about, of one employer that may be known to you.' The crowd of men laughed as they realised it was one of their workmates dressed up to look like their boss. And as he cavorted about the street imitating the mannerisms and facial expressions of their employer, Molly began to tell of that man's misdemeanours and inadequacies. How the crowd roared. Not only was their friend doing a grand impersonation of the poor boss, but now the tables had been turned, with Molly Albin listing all of his imperfections, as scripted by one of their own.

The show was met with such applause and hearty comment that it became the first of many to tread the streets of Hanley. And so, on one day Molly would be telling of those shameful men who had avoided work or were not meeting their family responsibilities. While the next she would be lampooning the very employer who had used her services the day before.

Not only did Molly bring her own style to the role of town crier, she was clearly a practical woman who had bills to pay and had few scruples over how she went about it. Very much like the hard-working Widow of Tettenhall … but she came to a sticky end, and that's another story.

The Tithe Pig

Now for a tale from the potteries themselves and not just the towns which surround them. The variety of pottery shapes, designs and uses to come out of this county has been immense and Staffordshire pottery is found all over the world, decorated with images from a myriad of folklore and mythology. As the artists sought to create new designs, they would not only look to classical myths, which added a cultured feel to their work, but also to more lowly stories – ones found in popular literature and the nation's oral culture. One such tale was that of 'The Tithe Pig', which made many appearances on Staffordshire pottery from the very early nineteenth century onwards. This story was often represented with the image of a parson and a humble farming couple, the man carrying a piglet and the woman holding up a baby. Occasionally, the woman was shown alone with the baby, pig standing behind her. Whether the woman faced the parson alone, or with her husband, doesn't really matter. Although the story can stand without him, I'll keep him in for this retelling.

There was once a parson who was rather rotund and jolly. Nothing unusual in that. He liked to laugh with his parishioners in the local tavern, enjoyed a good few of their risqué jokes and told a number himself. And why shouldn't he have been so contented and gregarious? The parson had everything he needed, and a little more besides, thanks to the most Biblical of practices – tithing. This was when each farming household within the parish was required to provide their priest with a tenth of whatever they produced, no matter how small. And the parson was diligent in ensuring that such a practice was maintained. The normally affable pastor would become the sternest pedant you had ever known whenever the day to collect the tithes came round. He would do his daily rounds of the parish, but this time there'd be no jokes or caring enquiry into one's well-being. Instead, he would stride into a house, with notebook in hand, and inspect all the produce, be it apples, grain or eggs, and set aside one tenth as required by Scripture, making due note of the precise quantity before arranging delivery or collection. And so the cupboards of the parsonage were kept full and its occupant well fed.

Now there was one young couple who knew it was the day for tithes to be collected and, like many others, had no real wish to pass on to the parson any of the produce they had worked hard to rear or harvest. Besides, they had ten children and needed every last morsel of food their limited efforts could provide. So it was with some resentment that they heard the news from one of their children that the parson was on his way up their lane.

The clergyman whistled as he walked up towards the house, allowing himself a moment of pleasure to consider the likely tithes he'd get from this family. He knew they reared pigs and so there would certainly be one tasty morsel here which he would be entitled to. Oh, the smell of succulent bacon cooking. His imagination had leapt into action with the thought of that tithe pig. He could almost hear the sizzling in the pan and taste the salty meat on his tongue.

The man and woman bemoaned and berated the approaching priest, trapped as they were by both tradition and Scripture. Until, the wife stopped suddenly in her grousing and a wry smile came to her face. She had an idea and one which she hoped would stop the parson from taking his tithe.

As the man of God lifted the latch of the gate, he pushed thoughts of a cooked breakfast to one side and took on a sterner countenance, so regaining his officious air. Striding up the path, he avoided the playful children with some annoyance. He almost tripped on some of the smaller ones as they chased about, asking him why he wore such a dark cloak and making rude comments about his wig. But the parson ignored them all. He was not going to be put off from taking that which he knew was rightfully his – a juicy porker.

The couple greeted the parson with a little more cheer than the previous tithe collections had brought, but the parson thought little of it. He pulled out his notebook and pencil, and then was led about the stores by the young farmer, noting all that had been harvested and what the tithe would amount to. The parson was pleased to see there were apples, which would set off the pork well, and a few bottles of wine. He wasn't so sure about these, but even if the nettle wine was no good, it would do as vinegar. It was when they returned to the yard and the parson saw such fine pigs that a smile almost came to his otherwise austere face. His thoughts turned again to the hiss and splutter of the frying pan and the rich aroma wafting to his nostrils.

It was at this moment that the wife appeared, carrying the youngest of her children. The baby was crying but the mother seemed to be doing little to calm it. 'Too many children,' thought the parson, 'the woman has become complacent.' But that child was making such a high-pitched grating noise. Not unlike a pig itself.

'You like our porkers then, do you, parson?' the encumbered mother asked.

'Indeed, madam, and I have made a note here of my tithe. I shall take that lovely specimen down there,' he said, pointing to an especially chubby piglet.

'Well, that's all well and good, parson,' said the woman. 'And you'll be taking this child as well?'

The parson was taken aback. Did that woman just ask him if he was going to take her baby?

'I'm sorry, madam. What did you say?'

'The child,' she said, holding the screaming baby up to the perturbed priest. 'This is the tenth child and so a tenth of our produce. All part of your tithe.'

The priest gave a nervous laugh. 'My good woman,' he spluttered, 'I don't want to take a child. How ridiculous!'

The woman suddenly took offence. 'What! Our tithe is not good enough for you?'

The parson attempted to put the woman straight; he said that his tithing was for harvested produce only, namely eggs, berries and pigs. But the woman forcefully impressed on the stammering man that a tithe was about *all* they had produced, their offering to the Church. Was he going to stop them from presenting what little they could to God? This family needed every blessing the Almighty was willing to dispense.

'No,' she continued. 'If you're going to take a tithe, you take a tithe of everything. None of your a bit of this, a bit of that. God requires a tithe and we're giving you a tithe. Take the baby or take nothing.'

And again she thrust the screaming child to the parson, attempting to place the red-faced baby into his arms.

The flustered man took a step back. He certainly did not want a child. How could he possibly take a shrieking monster back to live with him at his parsonage? He then became aware of the nine other children who had gathered around, all crying and pleading with him not to take their little brother away. He tried to explain that he was not going to take the child, but his protests were lost in the growing din. The mother was again pushing the baby towards him, the children gathering in closer. He tried to step back and tripped, stepping on the toe of one of the bigger ones, which made that one cry out. In haste the parson said he would not collect the tithe this year; that he could not take the child from its loving and expressive family. Then, making his way through the juvenile crowd as quickly as possible, he was out the gate and escaping down the lane.

Then the husband and wife laughed and laughed. The mother passed the baby to one of the older children, who gave him the milk that he so desperately wanted. They had got one over the parson, this year, and so would have plenty of bacon to go round. But what about next year? Who knows? Maybe, they'd have eleven children by then.

> In a country village lives a vicar
> Fond – as all are! – of tythes and liquor.
> To mirth his ears are seldom shut.
> He'll crack a joke and laugh at smut.
> But when his tythes he gathers in
> True parson then – no coin, no grin!
> The parson comes, the pig he claims.
> And the good wife with jaunts inflames.
> But she quite arch bow'd low and smil'd,
> Kept back the Pig and held the child.
> The priest look'd gruff, the wife look'd big.
> Zounds, Sir! quoth she, no child, no pig …

NED SAUNTERER

This is a fairly popular tale from the potteries and therefore one told many times, although some know the fellow as Sauntering Ned. It is a charming story and one I felt had to be included in this collection. As I have researched, I have found that in each telling of this story details are changed slightly, with various elaborations here and there. I cannot guarantee that the same has not happened with mine, but then that's how storytelling works. However, I believe that the story is based on a real person and a real event.

In the heyday of the Staffordshire potteries, there lived in Hanley a man named Ned. He was the sort who much preferred to doze under a tree in the sun than turn up for work. Who wouldn't? He much preferred the outdoors to being trapped all day in a factory or warehouse. Eventually, a day came when he decided to infuriate his boss no longer. Ned decided that he would leave the potteries and go travelling about. His plan was to take some pots, plates and bowls, which he would sell, and with the profits buy his next batch and so on. He was not a great entrepreneur, more the type who wanted to make enough money to get by and have every opportunity to enjoy the great outdoors. Of course, Ned soon found that to make just enough money to get by required working every day and a steady turnover of pots. So he began to travel about the county far more than he had first anticipated. It was an endless cycle of picking up pots and crockery, taking them to market, selling his wares, returning home, picking up more and setting off to further markets again. Yet despite all this, he would never rush and very soon he became a well-known figure about the place. Idly walking along with a donkey at his side and a small cart behind,

Ned Saunterer gained his name, and a friendly, jolly fellow he was known to be.

Some of the markets Ned frequented were a good distance from his home and there were times when he had to travel back in the darkness. It was not always safe to be out on those long roads alone, especially during the winter months. These situations worried Ned. What he needed was a cunning plan, something to deter any would-be robbers. As he sauntered along, considering various possibilities, all he could hear behind him was the clip-clop of the donkey's hooves. How he wished the beast would walk a little softer. The constant clip-clop was not giving him space to think. And then it occurred to him. That faithful donkey, always following him, was the answer. It accompanied him everywhere, so maybe he could make the most of this four-legged escort. Ned knew how superstitious many local people were and especially those robbers and brigands. Was there something he could do to make his donkey more fearsome? Something so that anyone waiting in the bushes lining a darkened lane would think a monster was approaching? Something which sounded like it had dragged itself out through the gates of Hell and into Staffordshire?

First, Ned attached a chain to the back leg of the donkey. His hope was that as the creature walked along the stony lanes and cobbled roads, the chain would scrape against the ground. He knew that the grating metallic sound would echo chillingly down the empty streets. Yes, he thought, that will sound not unlike the spirits of the dead rising up and rattling their hellish manacles.

His second plan was to make the donkey look more fearsome. After visiting those various markets, he had ended up with one or two curiosities, and one of them was a pair of horns.

He fixed these to some leather straps and made a peculiar head-dress for his donkey. After placing it around the animal's head, Ned stood back. The donkey looked at its master forlornly, but Ned was pleased with his creation. That long face crowned with two great horns would certainly look unnerving at night. The demon donkey, shadowed by the overhanging trees, coupled with the scraping chains rasping away, would mean that no would-be robber would be sticking around long enough to find out whether this creature was truly demonic or not. But how-ever proud he was of his handiwork, Ned could not allow wind of it to get about. If people knew what he had done then any element of surprise would be negated. So he kept the demonic costume hidden in a sack on his cart, only bringing them out for night journeys home, and he never told a soul.

An evening soon came when Ned needed to travel a good few miles from Cheadle Market to Stoke-on-Trent. It was a particularly wet November night and Ned was finding it hard going. So, he ensured that his donkey was done up in both the chain and the headdress. The last thing he needed was addi-tional hassle from any robbers or the like.

The two eventually came to the village of Bucknall and Ned needed to take a rest. It was not raining by then, so he sat in the village square without fear of simply getting wet. In fact, he was exhausted and it wasn't long until his eyes gently closed.

Ned was not sure how long he had dozed off for, but sud-denly a shouting woke him, breaking the sleepy silence of that darkened village. His eyes flashed open in time to see two men hurtling out of the churchyard and across the village square. They were screaming that they had seen the Devil and did not stop to take questions. Ned then noticed that his donkey was not beside him. He stood up quickly and listened carefully. Now

that the two men had gone, the village was quiet again. But he could not hear the sound of the scraping chain, which could have given him a clue as to the beast's whereabouts. He decided then that he should really take a look in the churchyard. Those two men had certainly been terrified by something, but would it really have been his donkey? Ned's ingenious donkey get-up was only likely to scare someone if they were in a darkened lane, where they'd be unlikely to get a good look. But then again, folk hanging about in graveyards would often be a bit keyed up and would probably be tricked by his horned donkey.

Gingerly glancing about the graves, Ned called out the donkey's name, but not too loudly. He didn't want to wake the dead. Edging about the corner of the church, he heard a munching sound. There in the moonlight stood his old donkey, feasting on some of the grass growing between the graves. He strode over to the animal, his relief dispelling any earlier fear. Then he saw that the grave beside which the donkey stood was open. Spades had been left on the grass, as if thrown to one side. As Ned looked at the unholy scene, it slowly dawned on him what had happened. Those men who had run screaming from the church must have been grave-robbers, or maybe even Resurrection Men. They had been digging up this grave and had entered the pit they had reopened. And who should have come across them, only Ned Saunterer's old donkey. What a shock those immoral chancers must have received when they looked up from within the grave – a long face looking down at them with a pair of horns, silhouetted against the moon. No wonder they ran from that churchyard like bats out of Hell, shouting and screaming that they had seen the Devil.

Ned shook his head, chuckling to himself. He never thought his donkey would be a deterrent for grave-robbers. He was about to lead his donkey back to the road, when he noticed that those men had left something else behind. It was a long wooden cart, ideal for carrying a coffin. They must have been Resurrection Men after all, he thought. Ned pondered for a moment about taking this unholy hearse on to the local constables, but then another thought struck him. Such a long cart would be able to carry far more pots than his old one ever could. So he quickly shifted the few pots he did have remaining that night. Then he fixed his donkey to the new cart, and following a hurried removal of the chain and the horns (they had done their job already that night), Ned continued on his way home.

Well, it didn't take long for Ned's fortunes to change. With all those extra items he was able to carry to market each day, his little business grew. It grew until he had a little more to do than he really cared for. Ned liked being out in the open, but still he didn't care too much for work. So he passed the business on to his sons and it kept them going for a very long time. Ned Saunterer still carried on with his donkey, taking pots and crockery about the place, but he returned to a small cart. He didn't want to be doing too much, not now he was getting older. He may have been known near and far as Ned Saunterer, but it wasn't till after he had retired that he began to tell of his 'Devil donkey' and the tale of when he gave those Resurrection Men the scare. 'Ah,' he said. 'They thought that Judgement Day had already come and the Devil was having his last skip about the earth. And all the time it was my donkey.'

The Blacksmith of Mucklestone

It was on St Thecla's Day, in 1459, that a woman of royal personage rode out of Mucklestone (pronounced Muxon) on her horse, as fast as she could. But the poor beast looked very uncomfortable, hobbling its way along the road to Newcastle-under-Lyme. The blacksmith of the village watched them go and looked down at the hoof prints in the soft sandy lane.

'Well, she was right,' he sighed. 'Those hoof prints are round the wrong way and I guess they could confuse your enemy. But I'm not sure how fast that horse is going to go.' And shaking his head, young William Skelhorn turned to go back to his forge. He had opened up for the Queen, and for a few others, even though it was a Sunday. He put the fire out and left hoping to enjoy the supposed day of rest.

William had not actually been to church that morning. He had heard of the battle over on Blore Heath and wondered if it was better to stay home and keep his head down. But a number of soldiers had come knocking on his door asking him to fix this pike or that breastplate and even shoe the odd horse. But all that was nothing compared to when Queen Margaret of Anjou had come a knocking.

The French queen had been watching the bloody battle from the tower of St Mary's Church, and as she stood in the damp she cursed her husband. Did she have to do everything for this supposed King, she thought. If only she had known before the wedding. Certainly, she knew there would be things to get used to. After all, she had hardly known the man and everything had been arranged. But she had not been prepared for a madman. How could such a man lead a kingdom when he burst into tears at the very mention of roses? Tensions had been growing right across England, and by then the houses of York and Lancaster were at each other's throats. And it had all led to this, the Battle of Blore Heath in Staffordshire. Margaret of Anjou watched the fighting carefully and could clearly see it was not going well for her Lancastrian men. She stood there fuming. She cursed her husband again. Then she cursed all the men of Lancaster. Then she cursed the erratic English weather. Her anger was so intense that some say her footprints remain in the stone floor of that tower.

Queen Margaret now had the measure of the battle, and she was not going to stay idle much longer. She was in Yorkist land as it was. If the House of Lancaster was going to lose, then she would have to make a quick escape. With her feet almost spinning over the stone steps of the spiral staircase, she headed down from the tower and out of the church. She continued outside the church-yard to where her horse was waiting. Skelhorn's forge stood nearby.

William had not put out the fire, just in case anyone else should call, but he was thinking that a pint of ale would be most welcome about then. Just as he went to leave, he halted suddenly. He'd almost bumped into Margaret of Anjou, who strode in leading her horse.

'Bon,' she said. 'You are ready for me. Shoe my horse.'

William sighed; more work.

'Very well,' he said and looked over the beast. It was already shoed and the iron was hardly worn.

'Non,' said the Queen, 'What I mean is remove the shoes and put them back on, but around the wrong way – front to back, back to front.'

William looked at her, confused. Had something got lost in translation?

'Yes, you heard right,' she snapped.

Never had he known this before. He wondered if she was going the same way as her husband.

'Imbecile!' she cried, 'Do as I say! There is no time to argue. Those Yorkies will be here in an instant. I must be on my way. With the horseshoes on the wrong way, any tracks I leave will show me as having headed off in the opposite direction. Have you never heard of such a trick?'

William had to admit he had never heard of such a thing and he wondered how the horse would take it.

'Never come across it before, your Majesty,' he said as he removed the pins as quick as he could. The woman was most insistent and she was Queen after all.

'Bon – then maybe the Yorkies will not have heard of it either.'

Working as fast as he could, the blacksmith removed the shoes and then reversed them as requested. Getting them to fit on the hooves again was a bit tricky and the horse didn't seem to like it. But soon he had reversed the shoes on all four feet.

Flinging the blacksmith a bag of coins, the Queen rose up onto her horse and then rode out of the forge. Then she sharply turned back to say one more thing.

'If anyone asks,' she whispered conspiratorially, 'I was never here.' So, William watched her head off down the road, and then turned back shaking his head. He really could do with that ale now he thought. Someone had to celebrate St Thecla's Day and anyway, it looked like there was going to be regime change in the country. What would that do to the price of beer?

The Mysteries of the Waters

Although there isn't a great tradition of stories associated with water in Staffordshire, there are a handful of intriguing tales about the various meres, lakes and pools scattered across the county. I have already told you about the Mermaid of Blackmere and how she threatened the local farmer with flooding, but there are a few other pools in the county where flooding was not only a reality, but considered fortunate. One is Hungry Pool at Billingham, which had a very unusual reaction to rainfall, quite opposite to normal expectations. If precipitation was to decrease so much as to create a drought, then the pool overflowed. The farmers would, of course, rejoice at such an occurrence and dig trenches to channel the water to their fields. But the wonder continued, because if rainfall was plentiful, then Hungry Pool lived up to its name, its water level dropping so low that it threatened to dry up.

Another which worked in a very similar way was Druid Mere at Aldridge, where the farmers would also channel the waters when drought came because it overflowed. But on another note there was Marshall Lake. It is said that this pool had such refreshing water that the local hunters would bring their tired horses to drink there. Very soon after they had refreshed themselves, the horses would not only continue with the hunt, but would spring into renewed action, ready to run as if they had not been out at all that day. Sadly, the location of this pool is no longer known. Imagine if they could have bottled it for selling! Such stories are reminiscent of Staffordshire's proliferation of healing wells and springs associated with the saints of Mercia … but their stories are told in earlier chapters.

One final pool to mention is found outside of Norbury and was known at one time for the vast number of birds it attracted. Despite being over 30 miles from the sea, seagulls were often seen on the island, which sat in the middle of the water. And of course lapwings, also known as peewits, were common there too. So it was named Peewit Pool. It was on the land owned by a family often known as Skrimgeour, although this name is now more commonly written as Scrimshaw. The keepers of the island would wait until the season's hatchlings had almost matured and then would set up nets on the banks surrounding the pool. Taking a small boat out to the island, they would drive the young birds off the land into the water and eventually into the nets. It was quite a job, with many of the birds flying off.

However, those that did fly away would very soon return to the island, such was their relationship with that lonely piece of land. The keepers then untangled the captured birds, taking them to be fed until they were plump enough to sell. It is said that they would sell over 1,000 birds each year. By the end of July, the rest of the colony would take flight, only returning in the following spring. However, all this changed the day Mr Skrimgeour died. It was as if the birds knew of the death and feared the next landowner, because they all flew off and did not return. The keepers looked out for them each spring, but none were seen here again. They had always returned in early March, but none were seen for the next three years. Was it that the birds had trusted the deceased proprietor only?

Then, after three years, the birds were seen again. They were not at Peewit Pool though. The birds now landed on another piece of land a few miles away. However, the proprietor's son, the heir of Skrimgeour, owned this land. Where the birds had been in those intervening three years, nobody could tell, but one of the keepers surmised that they must have been trying out all sorts of places until they realised that they were only happy on Skrimgeour's land.

ROBIN OF LOXLEY

It is intriguing to find a strong link with Robin Hood here in Staffordshire. I have heard that the area known as Sherwood Forest did, in fact, stretch so far that it touched the edges of this county. Albeit a 'forest' originally referred to an area of land designated for hunting and not necessarily a wooded area. And then Robin Hood is said to have been the Earl of Loxley before he was outlawed, and there is a Loxley not so far from Uttoxeter. In fact, the Kynnersely family of Loxley Hall are known to have a horn in their possession marked with the initials R.H. Is this the horn with which the man in Lincoln green would summon his Merrie Men? And in recognition of all of this, it seems, there is at Bramshall, not 2 miles from Loxley Hall, a pub named the Robin Hood. All of this may then be due to the old ballad 'Robin Hood's Birth, Breeding, Valour and Marriage'. Intriguingly, it tells of how the outlaw was in the county and married a young lady associated with Tutbury Castle. This was not Maid Marian, but another woman, and so I tell the tale of Robin Hood's first marriage.

The story begins at a time when all was well with Robin. His family had not yet been evicted from Loxley Hall and they would often travel about the area visiting various cousins in their grand houses. How different those times were from the ones he was to face as an outlaw, living in Sherwood Forest. At this time though, he would, with the other gentry, enjoy fine feasts, games and entertainments. Robin was known not only for his superior archery skills, but also his lust for life and how he would throw himself into the fun, leading many dances both new and old. It was on one of these occasions, at Christmas time, that Robin travelled with his mother to meet with the Gamwells of Gamwell Hall. Robin's mother was the niece of a Coventry knight whose name was Sir Guy. This was not that Guy of Gisborne of course, that would be another story. But in this tale, at Gamwell Hall, six tables were arrayed with delicious delicacies, such as mustards, meat and generously filled plum pies. George Gamwell himself, the master, gave a stirring speech to welcome his guests from Loxley Hall, and then the entertainments began. The Gamwells had a man in their employ who was proficient in many dances, games and tricks. His name was Little John and it was he who led the jollity that day. Robin was so impressed with this master of entertainments, and Little John himself was so encouraged by Robin's great enthusiasm to participate in the events, that the two of them quickly became firm friends.

But it did not stop there. The host, George Gamwell, was enthralled with Robin too, and, whether it was the ale talking or not, he turned to this young man of Loxley and asked him to come and live at Gamwell Hall. He even went on to promise that Robin would inherit his land once he passed away.

A little taken aback, Robin asked only that he should have Little John as his page. The squire was a little disappointed that Robin had not taken up his offer to live at the hall, but was pleased that he could do something for the young man and so gladly passed his entertainer on to this man from Loxley.

Robin and Little John then were inseparable and, as his page, John assisted Robin in all affairs to do with his archery, for this was Robin's greatest interest.

As winter turned to spring and fairer weather came to the land, Robin and Little John ventured out into the southerly edges of Sherwood Forest. Here Robin would take target practice and sometimes engage in a little hunting. Robin had been there many times and had made himself a humble hunting lodge from the branches of trees. He was known in the forest by many of the yeoman, who had a great respect for him, and they would come to his aid when he blew on his horn.

One day, when the two men were hunting, they wandered out from the cover of the trees onto the hills and there, before them, quietly meandering, was a flock of grazing sheep. As they came out into the open, a comely shepherdess caught Robin's eye. Not only did her beauty gain his attention, but he also noticed that she wore a pair of buskins which went up to the knees. Such boots were expensive, and not the usual footwear of those who worked with sheep. He surmised therefore that this young woman was of noble birth and perhaps only dallying with the care of sheep, a game perhaps to pass the time in an amusing way.

Robin strode over the little hill so that he could talk to this intriguing woman. As he gained on her, he saw more to interest him. Not only was she of a graceful gait, almost drifting over the hill, but in her hand she carried a bow not a crook, and a quiver full of arrows hung by her side, resting on her shapely hips. So now Robin's stride turned into a run, while Little John attempted to keep up.

'Fair lady,' Robin called, 'Fair lady, where are you going? Whither you away?'

She turned to face the man and smiled to see him running up the slope to her. Her black hair blew about her face as a breeze gently caressed the hillside and moved over her skin, which was as smooth as glass.

'Why,' she answered, 'I am hunting a fat buck.' And she looked cheekily down at Robin's waist with a smile. 'Tomorrow is Tutbury Day, good sir, and we must have a decent dish for these celebrations.'

Robin was taken with her beauty, and her voice betrayed her background, affirming those suspicions aroused by her long boots. She spoke in the sweetest tones, showing both guile and modesty in her words.

'I like to hunt as well. See my bow and my arrows,' Robin now continued with enthusiasm. 'And set within the trees I have a little lodge to service all my hunting needs. Would you care to take a look?'

The lady smiled and Robin felt the sun shine in his heart.

'I know the place of which you speak,' she said, 'but is that not the lodging of Robin of Loxley, the finest archer in our fair kingdom?'

'It is the abode of Loxley,' Robin confirmed. 'But as to whether he is an archer of such high skill I could not say.'

The lady raised one fine black eyebrow in surprise.

'Indeed, for I am he,' Robin whispered conspiratorially.

And then she laughed, her joy like a playful cascade tumbling out across those hills.

As Little John caught up with the flirting couple, he saw they had now turned towards him and were walking back in the direction of the woodland.

'Come on, John,' Robin laughed as he slapped his page upon the shoulder, 'Turn about now and join us as I show this lady my makeshift hunting lodge.'

So with a shake of the head and not a breath for words, the dutiful Little John turned and followed after the tittering pair.

It was as they entered the woods that Robin suddenly ceased from his charming and held up a hand. The lady and the page froze as Robin silently indicated something of distinct interest ahead of them. Through the trees, the sun shining golden on its back, stood a stag. Its great antlers were raised like the tangled branches of a tree, rivalling those of Abbots Bromley. Robin then winked at his fair companion, whispering how he would shoot this deer for her, provided that she came to the feast at Tutbury. Slowly he reached up over his shoulder for an arrow. Smoothly he lifted it from the quiver as he raised his longbow with the other hand. Then there was a twang and a rush of air as another's arrow sped past Robin's ear. The stag fell before them. A perfect shot.

But if it was not Robin who had taken that shot, who had? In the time it had taken that man of Loxley to pull his arrow from the quiver, the lady beside him had set her arrow, aimed, fired and hit her mark.

'Now,' she said, turning to her forest guide, 'it appears that Robin of Loxley is the finest *male* archer in our kingdom, don't you think?'

A host of birds fluttered out from the safety of the treetops as Robin's laughter echoed out. He had never met a woman like this before.

'What is your name? Surely you cannot be anyone other than Diana, the huntress of the ancients?'

The lady smiled at the compliment, but shook her head.

'Then which goddess are you?' demanded Robin, smiling.

'My name is Clorinda, dear Loxley.'

And so they took up the stag, or rather Little John did, and it was taken to Robin's bower in the woods. Here Clorinda was given refreshment as sweet conversation tumbled on between the two, until Robin could contain himself no longer.

'How sweet it would be, if Clorinda would be my bride!' he finally declared.

At this, the young woman blushed and silence reigned for an eternal moment in that wooded dwelling. Till finally, she looked up and holding, Robin's eye with hers of steely blue, she replied, 'I would be, with all my heart.'

Robin then in his excitement wanted to call a priest to have them wed immediately, but Clorinda bade him wait.

'It may not be so just yet,' she laughed. 'I must be at the Tutbury Feast. That is the reason I am here.' But as Robin sighed and looked downcast, she went on to say, 'If Robin of Loxley would come with me, then I will ensure he is a welcome guest.'

With this in mind, Robin called on Little John to prepare a brace of bucks to take along with the stag slain by the lady archer.

Robin's faithful page performed these tasks, but in his heart he was beginning to feel that changes were happening more quickly than he had hoped. He may have been Robin's page, but what of the friendship they have shared not so long ago? It appeared to be dissolving more rapidly than that morning's dew.

The road to Tutbury was not always safe and some referred to it as a treacherous journey, where the fear of attack hung on every corner, as if travelling a 'Staffordshire mile'. And it was whilst he took this passage that Robin learnt more of the meaning of this phrase, for eight ruffians leapt out from the trees upon the three. Robin leant over and slapped the hind of the horse on which Clorinda rode, causing it to gallop off, and thus removing his lady from this harmful encounter. And as two brigands turned to give chase to Robin's love, he swiftly showed how the finest male archer in the kingdom could protect the finest female; he dispatched two arrows, one for each of those coarse men whose bodies were soon lying in the gutter.

Little John was sat on the wagon, which carried all those vittles he had amassed to take to the Tutbury Fair. On seeing the gang appear, he cracked the whip to hasten the horse's pace. A couple were knocked to the ground, spinning as the wagon clipped past them, but four still managed to climb up and they began to help themselves to the food. Robin jumped off his horse and swung himself up onto the wagon too, where began a fight of shanks and flagons, loaves and hogsheads. That was until John pulled sharp upon the reins, bringing that mobile brawl to a sudden standstill. Two men fell and John dealt with them, whilst Robin continued with the last two on the wagon. John had thrown his two over the neighbouring hedges, where they landed on a rocky outcrop, near enough breaking their backs. All the while, Robin continued with the food fight. Then Little John marched over and, picking up his heavy quarterstaff, cracked the skulls of both offenders.

With the marauders finished, Robin and Little John looked at each other and smiled through puffs and panting.

'Good work there, Little John,' said Robin.

'We won't miss out on more times like these?' asked Little John.

'Of course not,' said Robin, climbing down off the wagon and looking for his horse.

'Even with Clorinda now on the scene?' Little John said meekly.

Robin stopped and turned to face his page and friend.

'We'll always have each other, John,' he said. 'Even if I get turfed out of my home and live forever in the woods!'

John snorted, 'Like that'll happen!' And he whistled to call back Robin's horse.

What rejoicing greeted the two men when they arrived at Tutbury Castle. Clorinda had told all of the attack out on the road and everyone was worried for the pair, not least Clorinda herself. And so the bagpipers and the fiddlers played with greater gusto and Robin's lady friend sang to celebrate her love's arrival.

> Hey, merrie men, with a derry-derry down –
> The bumpkins they are beaten good
> Put up thy sword now, Robin Hood,
> And we will dance on into town
> As merry men, with a derry-derry down.

And so the cheerful throng marched and sang down from the castle and into the town, where they met with those who were dancing a morris. These men had travelled down to the feast from Betley to share the beating of their sticks together with their tales and hodening. And on that day, the story of Robin's brawl alongside Little John became a part of that morris side's own repertoire, with songs composed and costumes improvised.

Little John, a former master of entertainments, came back into his own at the feast, with his dances and juggling. And Robin joined with his old friend to show the people of Tutbury how vigorously a feast could be enjoyed. Clorinda was in hysterics to see the charming archer she had met on the hills now performing jigs and clowning about with such humour and energy. And all drank a health to Clorinda, telling her that bold Robin of Loxley was indeed an amusing fellow, a very fine man, and how both he and John were such merry men together.

And so it was that when dinner was ended, a parson who was there that day, one Sir Richard of Dubbridge, was called forward. He brought with him his Mass book and, as the festivities quietened, a solemn moment was created. It was now that Clorinda held up her promise, and she and Robin were joined in holy matrimony. A roar then rose up from Tutbury and the celebrations took on a new lease of life. But despite his earlier horseplay, Robin took his sweet bride from the crowds. Climbing up onto their steeds again, the two now left the town to return to the seclusion of Robin's hunting lodge hidden in the trees of Sherwood Forest. As they entered hand in hand, the birds sung of the pleasures hidden by the leaves.

And Little John sat with the drunken gents of Tutbury, watching the morris men of Betley practise their new songs and stories of brave, strong Robin, hoping to catch some mention of one John Little with a quarterstaff.

THE CHAINED OAK

This is a story popularised by Alton Towers, being the premise of a ride named Hex. This tale has been so successful that many believe the theme park created it, and it is a genuine folk tale of old Staffordshire; however, their version isn't too far from the original.

It was on the carriageway known as Barbary Gutter that the Earl of Shrewsbury rode in his coach home from his weekly Mass at St Giles' Church in Cheadle. The church was freezing in those days and the Earl was looking forward to being back at Alton Towers where he would soon be sitting in front of a great roaring fire. It was late autumn and the golden leaves swirled about the coach as it made its way along the bumpy road, lit only by the lanterns on the carriage itself. When suddenly, it stopped. The Earl looked out, but it was so hard to see in the evenings at that time of year, especially under the shade of an old oak tree.

'Any change, Sir?'

There was a woman suddenly in his face. She carried in her hands a long, thick branch from the oak tree. He was used to such solicitation in town, but here on his own land? He shook his head and beckoned her onward.

'Nothing?' she continued. 'Not even for removing this branch from your path?'

How could she have moved something so large? She was a slight, fragile old woman. She obviously fancied her chances and was attempting to swindle him, even for a small coin. He ordered the coachman to continue and the carriage began to pull away.

'Know then, Earl of Shrewsbury, that every time a branch falls from this oak tree, a member of your family will die!' cried out the aged voice as the landlord resumed his journey home.

That night the winds howled about Alton Towers; winds that were strong enough to rip the branches off trees. And as the Earl attempted to sleep in his bed, the curtains wafting in a draught, the words of that old woman rang in his ears. He told himself it was just the moaning of the wind goading his imagination. But he was jolted upright by a sudden knock at his bedroom door.

It was his butler, summoning the Earl with the news that his elderly mother had suddenly passed away. Asking how he knew, the butler told the Earl that the maid had heard a clattering coming from the mother's room. The maid had taken the liberty of investigating and found the woman lying half out of her bed, no longer breathing. It was as if she had attempted to step out of bed to get someone and then lost her life.

The doctor was called but no foul play could be ascertained. She was an extremely elderly woman, so it seemed that her life had simply run its course. But the Earl looked troubled, for the clattering which had summoned the maid to the room turned out to have been the smashing of his mother's window. And pushing through the broken glass was the branch of an old oak tree. Had it simply been snapped off by that night's strong winds, and caught up in the gale to be carried to the window ,where its momentum caused it to break through the glass?

On the day of his grandmother's funeral, the Earl's son decided to go out riding. He missed her, despite some of her cantankerous ways. And so he saddled his horse and rode out along Barbary Gutter. It was as he was passing underneath that same old oak tree, that he heard the creaking sound of splitting wood. Suddenly, a branch fell down upon him. It missed him, but hit the horse across the back. Falling, the horse lay heaving atop the young man, pinning him to the ground. He cried out for help, over and over, until finally the gardener heard him. When help did arrive, it was too late for the horse. The Earl's son was dragged out from under the dead beast. Although his leg had been crushed, he hardly made a sound – only a soft whimpering. He was looked after, his leg eventually healing, but he then spent many weeks, maybe even months, simply sitting and murmuring to himself.

Distraught, the Earl strode out to that carriageway and stood defiantly under the tree. First it had been his mother and now almost his son. If it was magic, then he was stronger than any old woman's pronouncements. He wanted to show that clear thought and practicality would destroy the power of so-called curses. The Earl ordered that the oak tree be chained up. Every branch was to be held up and supported by every chain his men could lay their hands on. Not a single branch would fall from that tree again – curse or no curse.

To this day the unnerving sight of a tree held in chains remains, imprisoned for no fault of its own, simply that it was a tool in the curse over the House of Shrewsbury, a hex over Alton Towers.

THE THREE KINGS OF LICHFIELD

Three slain kings
Named Borrow, Cope and Hill,
When the battle was ended,
Lay quite cold and still.
Legs, arms and bodies
Were scattered all about,
For the battle had been cruel,
Of that there was no doubt.

Let me tell you of a time
When three kings ruled three lands,
Which met together in the place
Where Lichfield City stands.
Their names were Borrow, Cope and Hill –
And all three were Christian kings,
Living in communion
And agreement on all things.
And when those Romans marched up here,
They were surprised to find
There was not one, but three royal men
Who were to Christ aligned.
Now Diocletian, Emperor,
Despised our holy Lord.

All followers were put to death
By knife and flame and sword.
In fact, our dear own brave St George
Met his end this way –
His red blood on a bright white stone
Gave us our flag today.
So when word reached that Emperor's ear
Of these three British kings,
He ordered that they should convert
Or endure appalling things.
No invitations came from Rome
For them to see her glory,
As with so many other kings –
Theirs was a different story.
A deputation soon arrived
With soldiers hard but cunning.
They met with each king on his own
And told them things so stunning.
The soldiers stated to each K]king
A lie about the other,
Of how two had abandoned Christ,
To come to Rome as mother.
Now Borrow, he was not a fool,
Cope did not believe a word,
And Hill saw through the whole charade
As utterly absurd.
The three kings then arranged to meet
To confirm their own suspicions.
None had converted, they were right,
All three remained good Christians.
And so the three had met this way

The Roman news to test,
But those foes had been more sly
Than our three kings had guessed.
The soldiers knew the kings would meet
If given news this way,
And now they had three in one spot,
Then three at once they'd slay.
Borrow, Cope and Hill were done,
But as one man stood brave,
And down upon them Romans came –
Five thousand in one wave.

The blades, the shields, the spears, the cries
Continued without rest.
The three kings rose against their foes,
Their faith put to the test.
Their backs they formed a triangle –
A trinity were they –
Fighting with the Christ in mind
But each one fell that day.

The Romans looked about the scene
As silence had returned,
And what remained they gathered up
In order to be burned.
The pieces then of those three kings
Were found somehow to fill
Twelve baskets, which were then stacked high
Atop that battle's hill.
So with those remnants set alight
The fire quickly raged

And every soldier left the scene
Where martyrdom was staged.

And as the clock turns, so the years
And stories are passed down.
They called that place 'field of the dead',
And here there grew a town.
And from that phrase a new name sprung,
'Lichfield' it became –
And even though he won that day,
Diocletian has been shamed.
For at that place named Borrowcop Hill,
A cathedral has arisen –
Three spires pointing heavenwards
Show our three kings' one vision.

TALES FROM THE BLACK COUNTRY

As we approach the more southerly regions of Staffordshire, we enter that part of England known as the Black Country. Now, the Black Country is not solely a section of Staffordshire. Much like the Moorlands, this area is shared by two other counties. In this case, Warwickshire and Worcestershire. However, this region is definitely the industrial zone, in stark contrast to the sheep-farming nature of the Moorlands. In fact, as we journey from north to south across Staffordshire, the industry greatly increases. Of course, we had the potteries, but now we are in the land of iron and heavy mining. Again the name here is important, with 'black' referring to either the mass of coal mined or the smoke billowing from the factories and forges. It is curious to see how the Black Country has very much its own outlook and culture, drawing together these corners of Staffordshire, Worcestershire and Warwickshire. There has certainly been a merging of rural folklore and Mercian history with life in the urban, industrial world of the Victorian era. Fairies are here still, as is the Devil. There are giants and there is even a dragon, but all these mythic person-alities have a definite Black Country flavour, marking them out from the rest of Staffordshire. The Devil finds himself in a land which frightens him, whilst the fairies are up to the challenge, appearing more earthy and physical in this region. The characters in these stories embody much of the humour and attitude of this fascinating corner of England, as with the likes Aynuk and Ayli (Enoch and Eli). I could not talk about the Black Country without mentioning these two; they have been part of life here for generations. And their adventures just keep growing, being periodically resurrected to comment on current affairs and society's daily concerns, as only the people of the Black Country can. Not being from these parts, I have avoided recording or retelling their stories. I could not do them justice, but once you have read the following tales, look up this pair of pals. Their exploits and insights speak volumes about the insightful wit of wise fools.

THE DEVIL COMES TO THE BLACK COUNTRY

William Blake talks of 'dark Satanic Mills' and there certainly is a revulsion felt towards industrialisation in much of English poetry and Romantic literature. The Black Country may have gained from the rise of such industry, but it doesn't mean everyone liked it. Even Staffordshire folklore suggests that th'Olde Lad wasn't that fond of what they'd done with the place.

Noise, noise, noise! A barrage of strange and incessant sounds deafened Satan. But they were not in Hell. They were coming from the surface of the earth. In fact, the machinations of Hell were drowned out by the noise and th'Olde Lad decided that he had to have a look for himself. So up came that Devil, breaking out from the fiery pit to cast his eye about.

What he saw gave him a shock! He saw the great factories with their constantly revolving wheels, giant mechanical hammers beating, and people going about their work – back and forth like ants.

'I thought that we had created as diabolical an existence for any soul down below as could ever be imagined,' muttered th'Olde Lad, 'but looking about here I see black smoke thicker than a cloak of lies, flames so intense they would melt my horns, and my ears are met with such a hammering and pounding I'm afraid for my brains, that they will come tumbling out of my ears and my head will collapse.'

He then climbed up Brierley Hill to get a better look at the factories and forges. He could not believe that humans had created such pens to herd up their own kind, so crowded together and working with such overwhelming heat. Satan tutted, saying, 'I never more shall be amazed at Hell's fierce flames.'

He went on to Dudley Woodside and Bradley Moor, where the roaring of the forges thundered in his ears once more.

'I've heard a row in Hell,' he said, thinking of all the pounding his demons dealt out, squashing the souls of humanity for all eternity, 'but I've known none like this.'

In fact, the longer the Devil was in the Black Country, the more his nerves were assaulted and the more flummoxed he became. He ran on to Sedgley, but couldn't stop in that relentless din. He had to charge through holding his ears, the clopping of his hooves on the cobbles barely audible over the racket. On and on the Devil went, crying out, 'Is there no end to this pandemonium!' But none answered, for none heard him. 'This has to truly be the most hellish place that creation has even known,' he bewailed.

'What can I do? What point is there to my existence, when Hell seems a child's fairground ride compared to this ungodly wilderness?' And there at Stanton, the Devil cried and moaned and ground his teeth, such was the noise that went on and on. Until, the Devil threw himself in anguish onto the unforgiving stone. With full force, he crashed against the rock-hard ground, breaking every bone in his body and th'Olde Lad was no more … for a while.

THE WIDOW OF TETTENHALL

The Church of St Michael and All Angels, Tettenhall, is a fascinating place and well worth a visit, especially to see some of

its more ancient carvings. The lintel stone bears the date 1686, but its carved figures look much older, almost pre-Christian. However, in the graveyard there is another curious sight. There, almost hidden by the grass, lies a gravestone which appears to have been carved with the figure of a woman, but she has no arms or legs. Local tradition states that the stone moves a little each year, closer and closer to a certain tree standing in the graveyard. There is no name inscribed on it, but there are many stories about the woman that it could be a memorial for. Some say it was a gypsy woman, others say a seamstress. I will therefore tell one of the tales which works best as a complete story, but I would encourage you to visit Tettenhall yourself. Ask about and see what other explanations you can find for this enigmatic gravestone.

There was once a widow woman who had to work hard each day to make some kind of living, having no children to look after her. She therefore took on whatever jobs she could find, and was soon known for her sewing and spinning skills. Many of the locals would bring her clothes to mend or wool to spin; all the little jobs that they did not have time for. But it was never enough money for the widow. Payment for such work was minimal and she had no other skills to demand a higher fee. She would therefore use every hour that God sent, bent over in the poor light with needle and thread, or spinning away, her ankle asking to rest from all the pedalling. Now, in order to ensure that she had enough money to see her into the week, the woman did something that many others thought despicable. She would often work on a Sunday. This was, of course, the Lord's day, the Sabbath, and to work on such a day was defying a command from God. Her absence in church on Sundays was noted. When she did manage to come she was often late and the tut-tutting worshippers knew why this was – she had been working in the morning before the service. It was true. She would try to get to church by rising early to do her sewing chores, but then she'd hear the church bells and have to hurry a job, which often meant mistakes and some unpicking, and the poor widow would end up late again.

It was decided then that the vicar should go to see her; to admonish her in her avaricious ways so that she might learn to use this day of rest in the way that the good Lord had intended.

Now, when the learned priest went to the widow's house, he was ready to make her clear on how God had set aside one day of rest and to speak to her of the dangers of her love of money. He had Scriptures and examples ready to present to her and felt that he would surely bring this woman to repentance. She would again be a regular churchgoer and one who made her attendance on time. However, despite the woman having little in the way of education, she certainly knew why she did what she did and was not going to be pushed about by someone who clearly did not understand her situation. The discussion grew to be quite heated until, the vicar finally said that if she did not attend then there would be no help for the woman from the church. Now the help she did receive was little and not often, but the widow could not turn down any money to help ease her situation, no matter how small the amount. And so, suddenly, her attitude changed and she began to be more open to the idea of attending church regularly, on time, and not working on the Lord's day. So much so, that in her sudden ardour, she vowed that if she should work on a Sunday again then her arms and legs would drop off.

A few weeks passed, and to everyone's amazement the widow was seen in church, on time, and she was not seen spinning or sewing. However, each week the widow saw the pile of clothes that needed mending in her house and the wool that needed spinning, and she felt the pinch in her purse. It was hard for her to go out to church each Sunday and to then come home to see all that work waiting for her; work that she could not touch until Monday morning. But then, she had an idea.

It was on a Sunday morning, as the bells of St Michael and All Angels called the faithful to worship, that the gathering congregation saw a sight they had not expected. There, in the graveyard, sat under the tree, was the widow. She had with her not only a pile of clothing which she was mending with her needle and thread, but her spinning wheel was there also. The shocked parishioners tut-tutted and hurried into the church to tell the vicar, who came out amazed and appalled to see such industry taking place on sacred ground and on this sacred day. The woman explained that she was attending church. She would be able to hear the vicar's mellifluous tones as he read the liturgy and spoke his homily. She would hear the congregation and she knew the hymns well enough to join in without a book. Yes, she could work out here and still be part of the service, maybe even pop in to take the bread and wine of the Eucharist. It was this idea which enraged the vicar the most. How dare she suggest she could 'pop in' to partake of the body and blood of our Lord!

Now I have already indicated how she was not a woman to be pushed around, and so dismayed was she at the vicar's reaction that the widow then told him what she really thought. With much blasphemy she cursed the vicar, his church and all the members of that disingenuous congregation. But she had pushed it too far. In that moment there was a loud crack of thunder and from the heavens came a bolt of lightning. It hit that headstrong woman square on, with her arms and legs being expelled from her body. The vicar stood amazed, but justified.

A funeral was held for the dismembered widow and a rough gravestone was cut out for her by the son of the local stonemason. He had made it with arms and legs, not being an unkind boy, but many of the locals complained, saying that her end should be a lesson to all who put work before the grace of God. And so the stonemason chipped off the arms and legs, so that the stone only showed the head and torso of the blasphemous woman.

Her stone remains in this state, not far from Lime Tree Walk, in the graveyard of Tettenhall Church. And each year it moves a little, a tiny slide towards the tree where that widow worked. Maybe she's thinking still of all those clothes she left there that needed mending.

THE BLACK COUNTRY FAIRIES

For many people the classic image of fairies is that of delicate little people dancing in rings, dressed in soft flowing clothes fashioned from petals and feathers. That is not to take away from the powerful magic these tiny people possess, but the delightful dancing often belies not only a more mischievous side to these people, but a quick temper and perhaps even a belligerent nature. Many miners of the Black Country would talk about how their candles and picks had been stolen or moved by the fairies. And whenever a miner heard a mysterious knocking, he would move out of the mine as quickly as possible. It was either a fairy trying to weaken the roof or one giving a warning that a shaft or cavern was about to collapse. Those fairies that gave out the warnings were known as 'knockers' – an amusing name if you're not hundreds of feet underground. But despite the helpful attitude of some, you don't want to get on the wrong side of fairies. After all, they were the first to populate this island on which we live. Yet we humans treat the land as if we are the only ones who use it. It was down Churchery way that the little people would meet in the dusky sunlight to play their tinkling music and dance in their fairy circles. This had been the way for longer than any human could possibly remember, and the nightly meetings had gone on pretty much unhindered for centuries, if not millennia. However, if there is one thing to upset a fairy gathering, one thing that will scupper their magic, it's holy water. None of the humans living about Churchery had seen the evening gatherings of the fairy folk, although some were pretty certain of their presence in the area. So, in deciding where to build a church, the people of that village inadvertently chose the very same shady meadow where the fairy dancing took place. Before the building could begin, a consecration had to take place. A priest was brought to the site and he began chanting and reciting prayers, whilst sprinkling copious amounts of holy water.

When the sun slid down, the fairies crept out from their hidey-holes and gathered as they had always done, but, unbeknownst to them, the ground was sodden with holy water. It was hard to notice any additional dampness because fairies tend to prefer the wetter meadows, but they soon became aware that something was different. Their pipes began to squeak as they were played. Strings snapped on their fiddles. The odd dancer slipped in the middle of a spin or skip, whereas before they had been able to carry out these simple moves without a single worry. That first night, the fairies put it down to simply being a bad day. Perhaps they all needed a good rest, they thought. And they resolved to try again the next day.

The next day, however, the human builders arrived at the meadow, bringing with them wagonloads of stone. Their loads were emptied onto the site, leaving what amounted to great mountains in the eyes of the fairies. Some fairies said that they could still dance there, but they experienced the same problems as the evening before. Also, now there were stones in the way and chips of rock, which pierced through their delicate shoes. A sorry band of fairies hobbled away from the meadow that night.

The following day, the builders were back and began to dig out the earth where they would set the foundations for the church. And as dusk fell, the fairies returned to see their former gathering place destroyed. Great trenches now ran across it, as well as the enormous piles of stone from the day before. The holy water still resided in the ground and many of the fairies were beginning to feel sick and lethargic every time they came onto the old meadow. They all knew something terrible was happening and decided to wait up till morning to see what was going on.

Morning came and the builders arrived. They continued their work of digging, and then began moving the stones, placing them in the trenches to set down the church foundations.

The fairies now knew what was happening. It was perfectly clear and they didn't like it. They left the men to carry on with their building work – for now – and sped away, hopping over the stones and running into the neighbouring woodland.

As the sun lowered in the sky and the workmen called it a day, an army of fairies poured out of the woods. Like a sea of locusts, they swarmed over the stones and onto the foundations. The Churchery fairies had brought with them their cousins and second-cousins and even those several times removed, all to assist them in taking back their meadow for dancing. The holy water had weakened their magic, but with enough of them together, they were able to counter its effects and reclaim this land for themselves.

Another morning arrived and the workers turned up at the meadow to continue their work, but they all stopped and stared dumbfounded. There was nothing there. A number of them rubbed their eyes, a few blasphemed (forgetting the nature of the project they were working on), and all were truly flummoxed. There, before them, was the old meadow as it had always been. There were no piles of stones, no deep trenches and no foundations. Where had it all gone? And how had anyone removed all the rubble, filled in the holes and returned the place to its original state? In a daze, the would-be builders wandered about the former site, shaking their heads. The priest was sent for and was initially at a loss, until he spied a tiny pipe on the floor. Picking it up with only his forefinger and thumb, he held up the tiny instrument for the workmen to see.

'Fairies,' he said. 'The Little Folk have been here.'

'Been here and removed our church?' asked one of the men amazed.

'It seems that way,' replied the priest, looking about the place, 'but where have those mischievous imps put everything?'

A search was then on, but it was no 'hunt the thimble'. These men were looking for enough stone to build a church's foundations. How on earth could such a collection be hidden? It wasn't long until the whole community was drawn in and the search moved out from the meadow into the woods. And all the time, tiny eyes were watching and barely audible giggles were stifled.

Eventually, a boy came running over to the meadow. He was the son of one of the builders, and he was shouting that he had found the missing stones; not just the stones, but the missing foundations. Intrigued, a band of workmen, led by the boy's father and the priest, were taken through the woods, all the way to the town of Walsall. And sure enough, there were the church's foundations. In a field, a rectangle of trenches had been neatly dug out. Within the trenches, stone had been shaped and piled up, forming the foundations. A number of builders again rubbed their eyes and some were careful to ensure the priest didn't hear their blasphemies. Not only had the stones been removed and trenches dug, but the foundations were complete and set with a craftsmanship the workers had not seen before. Although, none of them said it out loud.

It would, of course, have been too much rigmarole to take out the stone and haul it over to Churchery to start the building of the church again. Even the priest had to admit that, but he wasn't happy with the foundations being placed on unconsecrated ground. So building work was delayed further as the priest spent another day chanting and praying and sprinkling holy water.

The fairies in the bushes had seen enough. They may not have been the biggest fans of holy water, but they knew that this meant the church was staying on the new site they had found for it, so they were happy. They flitted away, spinning with laughter through the air, to dance on the restored meadow at Churchery.

The church at Walsall remains. It's known as St Matthew's and is said to have been placed there by the fairies. They say you can still see the fairies dancing up at Churchery, despite all the building that has taken place since those days. But that's probably due to the fact that no holy water has been slung about around there. Those people of Churchery and Walsall should have told a few more of their neighbours about these incredible happenings, because much the same thing happened at Bilston and Wednesfield. People really should be more careful about where they're building. And so, the fairies of the Black Country continue to dance in their sweet, innocent way, but woe betide any who try to mess with their meadows again.

DICK THE DEVIL

There was a miner in Ettingshall who was known as Dick the Devil, because of the speed at which he worked. Somehow, he managed to turn out almost twice as much as anyone else. He wasn't particularly well-built and certainly wasn't the most energetic man down the pit, but each day he appeared to have worked as the Devil, his haul dwarfing those of the other men.

Each of the men were assigned different faces to work from, but Dick's was hidden from the view of all the other miners. Which was a good thing because he had a secret.

It had come about when Dick had heard one of the knockers. Instead of being scared, as the other miners were, Dick was curious. He wanted to find out exactly where the sound was coming from and whether it was the fairies. So, following the tap-tap-tapping sound, he crept up through a narrow channel in the rock. And as he pulled himself up to peer over a stony ledge, he saw before him a small crowd of little people chipping away at the stone. Reaching out with his hand carefully and quietly, he managed to grab one of the tiny workers. The fairy was so shocked to be nabbed in this way, that he pleaded with Dick not to harm him or his workmates and went on to promise that they would help him in his mining. Dick was a cunning fellow and could see the great advantage to be had in employing a team of fairy folk and so accepted their offer. Only the fairies had one more condition. Dick was not to tell any human how he came to produce so much coal, nor was he allowed to give even the slightest hint that he had had help from fairies. Dick agreed as he thought of all the extra money he would receive for the great amounts of coal he was soon to generate.

Each day then, as Dick casually chipped away, the fairies frantically worked with their little hammers, sweating away to give Dick the greatest haul, and to ensure that he was on their side. However, with all the extra pay Dick the Devil was earning, the other miners wanted to find out about his secret. He was, of course, very cagey about his methods. He certainly did not allow his colleagues to see him at work. Until one day, when everyone was hard at their posts, a certain miner crept over to Dick's corner to have a look. Peering over the rock he was amazed to see the tiny hammers sparkling in the candlelight and the host of little people working hard for Dick, who sat tapping at a stone without much effort. The miner couldn't resist calling out to Dick, having discovered his secret. But his cry alerted the fairies, who dropped their hammers and leapt into the air squealing and shouting. Thrashing about the cave like a maniacal swarm of locusts, their turning and spiralling grew faster and faster, as they whizzed past Dick the Devil's face time and time again. Until, suddenly, they all screamed an ear-splitting cry in unison. The dumbfounded miner watching it all covered his ears. The walls of the coalface began to shake as a ball of raging fire exploded out from nowhere. Bursting through the cavern, its comet-like power not only knocked that miner off his feet, but sent panic rocketing through the mine as the other workers dropped their tools and ran.

The flame did not last, however. The fireball quickly fizzled out to a small spinning spark on the ground. And so once the men had recovered from their ordeal (one of them stamping on that spark), they all cautiously crawled over to where Dick had been stationed. Peering again over the rock, the miners saw no fairies; only Dick without so much as a singe on him. Yet he was lying on the floor, still as the stone itself. Scrambling down into the cavern, the miners gathered about the man, one or two gingerly touching Dick's cold body. He had not been burnt, but there was no longer life there. That fireball must have come from the fairies' combined anger and so, for allowing another human to see them, Dick was dead.

The fairies were never seen down in those mines at Ettingshall again, but no one forgot what had happened to Dick the Devil. To those miners, this was a warning of what can happen if you get mixed up with fairies. A mistake none of them would make again – but that did not stop a shiver running down the spine of any who heard a mysterious tap-tap-tapping down there in the deep, dark mines.

THE DARLSTON PIG

There was once a man of Darlston who would never go hungry. The folk thereabouts always knew whether he was in or not, because if he was home then there was always the smell of cooking bacon wafting out of his cottage. Few are they who can resist the salty aroma which they say is enough to turn any vegetarian. And when those folk of Darlston caught that delicious smell, any passing would find some excuse to knock on the door. Their hope was that they would be invited in to share in the odd rasher or two. And this man of Darlston was always so generous to his spur-of-the-moment guests, serving up not only one or two, but maybe three or four, rashers of bacon. Now, however much you may like bacon, it is even better with an egg or a sausage or a slice of toast, but this man of Darlston never seemed to offer any of those. He would eat these other foods himself, sat there at the table with a full English breakfast, but it was only with the bacon that his generosity seemed to know no bounds. After a while, his neighbours noticed his peculiarity with the bacon and wondered why that was. They weren't complaining, but they knew very well that he only had one pig and five or six chickens. That pig had been with him a good number of years too. So where was he getting the bacon from? And why was he not as generous with the eggs?

The truth was that this man of Darlston had acquired the pig from the fairy folk. He had stumbled on a hidey-hole of theirs under a tree and, to keep him quiet, they had given him a pig from their own world. Now, to the untrained eye, a pig from the kingdom of fairies looks like any other pig, but its qualities are far superior. A pig from the fairy world does not have to be killed to give its owner bacon. The fairies had shown our man of Darlston how to call the pig with a high whistling sound, and on hearing this the creature would come, jump up onto the table and lie still on its stomach with its legs spreadeagled. It would then go into a sort of trance, during which anyone could take a knife and cut slices of bacon from the pig's body, with no blood spilling, and no damage to the pig at all. Then when they were done, all one needed to do was clash the knife and fork together three times and the pig would awake. It would leap off the table as if nothing had happened and live another day, to provide bacon whenever it was required again.

And so the man of Darlston had bacon in whatever quantity he required, which meant he could be as generous as he pleased. It was a different story with the chickens. They weren't magic and weren't good layers either.

SPRING HEEL JACK

The character of Spring Heel Jack is, to me, one of the most curious of Victorian Britain and he seems to have lodged himself quite firmly in the imagination of the people of the Black Country.

It was in the nineteenth century that tales started to spill out of London, reporting an unusual and dangerous fellow who would attack young women in dark streets. He was said to have a sharp, pointed face with a tightly clipped beard. He would often be wrapped in a cloak, which seemed to be attached to his wrists and ankles, so giving the appearance of wings. And his hands had long, bright claws with which he would rip through the clothes of his victims. However, despite the deep trauma his attacks must have caused, he does not seem to have actually killed anyone. Often the victim would scream and the bizarre attacker would leap away, up onto the roofs of the nearby houses, springing from one height to another, before disappearing into the darkness of the night. And so a phantom was born: Spring Heel Jack.

Stories of this frightening and perplexing character spread around the country and sightings were reported all over. Yet, in the Black Country, it wasn't a lone young woman who claimed to have seen the high-leaping villain. It was, in fact, a great crowd of people that saw Spring Heel Jack, all gathering together to watch him leap over the rooftops of Old Hill.

It began as the butcher of the town went to bed one evening. He had to be up bright and early the next day for a delivery, and so retired to bed early. However, as he tried to settle down, he was disturbed by what he thought were footsteps on the roof. Perplexed, and a little annoyed, he jumped out of bed and leant out of his window to shout at whatever impertinent youth had decided to clamber about on his tiles. But his cry of anger suddenly changed to one of fear as a pointy bearded face looked down at him from over the gutter and sneered. Then the figure leapt off the roof and in one single bound cleared the street to land on top of the pub opposite. The frightened butcher recognised the bounder immediately. 'Spring Heel Jack!' he cried. 'Spring Heel Jack!'

His voice echoed down the street and people emerged from every doorway, and started piling out into the street. Some came armed with pots and pans to beat the brute away, whilst others simply turned out to see this alarming wonder for themselves.

And then it seems that Spring Heel Jack put on a show for the gathered crowd. Instead of speeding away, as the stories often told, he bounced from roof to roof, skipping from chimney to gable, almost flying back and forth across the street. The crowd watched with cries and screams, uncertain whether to be scared or amazed, but eventually the gymnastic felon disappeared behind the rooftop of the shop at the end of the road. Some of the youngsters ran around the corner to see more, despite warnings from their parents – but they needn't have worried, Spring Heel Jack was gone.

After that time, reports of Spring Heel Jack were still heard across the region, but all were isolated sightings. None featured great crowds, like those that night in Old Hill, but the stories continued for several years afterwards. Occasionally rumours would circulate that Spring Heel Jack was back and people would keep an eye out for him, gathering outside the pub to spot him should he come leaping over the rooftops again. The landlord was pleased, and he may have been instrumental in setting the rumours going, but the leaping phantom was not seen this way again.

It was not long then until Spring Heel Jack joined the likes of Rawhead-and-Bloody-Bones and Dumb Baw, becoming one of the many bogeymen called on by Staffordshire parents to frighten their children. And these warnings were soon strengthened, as Spring Heel Jack was seen again. Not cavorting above the streets this time, but in the misty evenings along Staffordshire's canals. Bargemen would tell of how, as the sun was setting, they would occasionally see a figure leaping over the canal ahead of them. By the time they reached the spot, he was nowhere to be seen of course (barges not being the fastest of vessels), but it would seem that Spring Heel Jack moved out into the countryside. For many years, people would gather on the cinder paths along the canals in the hope of catching a glimpse of the diabolical acrobat once more. But it looked now as if he preferred to avoid the crowds. Whoever he was, or is, Spring Heel Jack has managed to leap into the mythology of Staffordshire and firmly keep his place there: a shadowy figure leaping the canals and hopping about in the minds of all who hear of him.

THE HAND OF GLORY

In Walsall Museum there is a display of a child's arm, which is known as the Hand of Glory. This phrase often refers to the hand taken from a hanged man. The hand was removed after death before being pickled and salted until it became hard. Meanwhile, a candle would be fashioned out of the dead man's fat, before being placed into the hand to make a lantern of sorts. Burglars were said to use the grisly candleholder when entering a home. It possessed a charm which was able to keep the occupants of the house asleep until the flame of the candle was blown out. However, the Hand of Glory at Walsall seems to be very different, if not equally mysterious.

The White Hart Inn at Caldmore Green was built in the 1600s and is one of the oldest brick buildings in Walsall. Even early on in its history it was gathering stories. It is said that a pear tree used to grow in its garden and would flower in both summer and winter. Others talked about how Queen Henrietta Maria, the wife of Charles I, had come to stay here. But by the eighteenth century there was talk of the inn being haunted by the ghost of a girl. Some say she had died through suicide, others say it was a cruel ritual killing, but either way, the girl's spirit was not at ease. Some said they heard soft steps walking across the attic when they knew that no one was up there. One person mentioned how they had discovered an unexplained handprint on a table kept up in the attic. For others, there were footsteps in the passageway.

One night, after the pub had closed, someone on the street outside, rushing home on a cold windy night, happened to glance across at the White Hart and gasped. There, hanging in the window, was a severed child's arm. Many laughed off these stories, but those who had heard the footsteps and knew the stories said that the arm had been cut off as part of the bizarre ritual that had taken place in the building many years before.

It was finally in 1870, when some workmen were fixing the chimney breast in the attic, that two objects were discovered behind some loose bricks. One was a sword from the seventeenth century, quite clearly the weapon of an officer of the Civil War. The other was a child's arm, complete with the hand. On analysis it was found to be a girl's arm and one that had been removed with extraordinary proficiency. People said that this discovery proved the stories of the ritual killing, as many atrocities were known to have taken place during those dark days of the English Civil War. However, the removal of the arm may not have meant an end to the strange goings-on at the White Hart, even though it has now been converted into a block of flats.

The Giants of Staffordshire

Staffordshire seems to have produced its own fair collection of giants over the years. One example is Edward Bamfield, who was known as the Staffordshire Giant. Despite this, no one seems to know exactly which part of Staffordshire he was from or how he came to move down south. Perhaps he was spotted – not hard being so tall – and someone thought they could make some money with a chap of his size. Or perhaps it was his own decision, having heard of Walter Parsons, another Staffordshire man of great stature who bettered himself by uprooting to the capital. Either way, he was living in London in the eighteenth century and he may very well have first appeared at the sideshows around Fleet Street. Here, both performing giants and performing dwarves were especially popular, and there is a picture of Edward in which he is standing with a Mr John Coan, also known as the Norfolk Dwarf. Later, Edward seems to have made a more celebrated name for himself at Covent Garden in the role of the Dragon of Wantley. At 7ft 4in, he must have been quite an impressive sight – a truly fearsome dragon. He played this part for almost six years before stepping down in February 1768. He sadly died the same year aged thirty-six. He was included in a painting by Charles Maucourt. Entitled 'Mirth and Friendship',

Maucourt's picture shows six men enjoying conversation together with some tobacco and a drink in a tavern. At the back of the crowd there is one who is of greater proportions than the other men, said to be Edward Bamfield.

Another giant Staffordshire migrant was Walter Parsons, a blacksmith who stood about 7ft 6in – a little taller than Edward Bamfield. He travelled to London more than a century before Bamfield to take up a much weightier role.

As the Earl of Buckingham was riding through Staffordshire, his horse became lame and he finally had to stop at West Bromwich. He found a blacksmith to tend to this and was intrigued to see a young giant of a man working the forge alongside all the other workers. He was able to work at the anvil due to a trench, which had been dug into the ground. Standing in the hole, which went up to his knees, the young man was just the right height for striking the iron. The Earl looked about and spoke with the blacksmith. He discovered that the giant's name was Walter Parsons and that there were also other trenches in the floor of the workshop so that he could get on with all the other jobs alongside his more diminutive workmates. Now, not only was Walter an impressive height, but due to the nature of his profession he was also well-built; he reminded the Earl of the stories of old, of giants from the adventures of King Arthur. And this gave him an idea.

When the Earl finally began his journey back to London, a grand guardian accompanied him. He had convinced Walter to come with him to meet the King, where he was sure he could provide James I with a bodyguard likely to deter any would-be assailant. Many would have wondered at the sight of the Earl of Buckingham riding on his horse beside the Staffordshire blacksmith. An image which would have looked as if it was straight out of a child's storybook.

On his arrival at the royal court, James I was amazed not only at the height of this young man, but also his breadth of stature. The King had seen tall men before. There had been John Middleton, the Childe of Hale, who was over 9ft tall, but the King had to agree with the Earl of Buckingham that this Walter certainly looked to be a formidable guardian. And so in a matter of weeks, Parsons went from small-town blacksmith to royal porter. Despite the hopes for him being able to see off any attacker, Walter was known for being more of a gentle giant. His manners and tender nature endeared him to many in the royal entourage. However, it was whilst walking round London itself that his patience was pushed. One particularly rowdy Londoner took to chasing after Walter, calling him for all sorts until Walter could ignore him no longer. He grabbed the churl by his breeches and the sudden lift up into the air knocked the wind out of the loudmouth. But Walter wasn't finished yet. The two of them were located in a street known for its butchers and, spying an empty hook, the King's porter hung up his victim, the hook piercing through the back of his breeches. And there the stunned name-caller was left, to endure the raucous laughter of all the stallholders and their customers.

But the stories of giants in Staffordshire go back earlier than these two. There is a tale of a conflict with their own up here in the West Midlands.

There was once a giant who had a beautiful wife, one who dwelt in the land of humans.. He had not stolen her or forced her to marry him. It had been her choice and in fact she had found him.

This young woman had always been different to other girls. For starters, she wasn't really interested in any of the young men who lived in her village of Kinver, or any thereabouts. But that wasn't really what made her different. There are, after all, many girls who are careful about the men they bring into their lives. Choosy some say, others say wise, but for this young woman it was something quite different. She had a secret that she knew would be feared by most ordinary people, and so the man she chose to marry would need to be one that she was sure would be able to protect her.

Now, she had heard that there were giants living in the nearby hills, which surrounded the Royal Forest, and although many spoke of how dangerous these people were, some had talked about kindly giants too. So she left her home to see for herself, in the hope of finding a husband she could genuinely trust to protect her.

She was gone for over a year and many of the young men of Kinver rued the fact that they had not made more of court-ing her when she was in the village. The girls wondered what it was that she thought made her so special. And many of the elderly folk simply commented that there had not been a thun-derstorm for at least twelve months.

So, some fourteen months later, the girl astonished everyone when she returned to Kinver carried in the arms of a young male giant. They were even more amazed to hear that this was her husband, and were all quite flummoxed as to how the two of them could possibly have a life together.

The giant greatly loved his diminutive wife and decided that he would prove to her his deep affection by building the perfect house for her. Firstly, he took an old metal horse trough, which he bent about to make a kind of spade, and sharpened its edges. Then, with this implement, he began to dig into the local stony landscape – Holy Austin Rock. Scraping away at the sand-stone, he soon made a number of chambers with windows and doorways. Then he began to gather trees and old bits of carts to make furniture for his wife. Some said it was like a father lovingly building his daughter a doll's house. But whatever they said, he had soon made for his wife the most charming stone cottage any had ever seen and she loved him all the more.

Now, over and beyond the nearby village of Enville, there was another giant. He lived in the rock fortress now known as Samson's Cave. It was in that year that Staffordshire experienced a drought and the giant, Samson, was soon without water. So, he went lumbering over the few short miles between Enville and Kinver in search of water, carrying a huge bucket in his hand. He knew of the stream dripping down from Kinver Edge, and so it made sense for him to fetch what he needed from here. He had come early in the morning knowing that if too many humans saw him there could be trouble.

Placing his bucket under the dripping water, at what is now known as the Giant's Water Trough, Samson waited for it to fill. As he did so, he idly looked about and saw the pretty little home created by the Kinver giant. Samson was intrigued to see such a creation and admired the colours of the flowers which grew about its door and windows. But the beauty of such things was nothing compared to that of the young woman he spied through the window, sleeping as if in a fairy tale upon her bed. As quietly as a giant may, he tiptoed up to the window and gently prised it open with his fingernail. She was certainly a most attractive young lady and he could not resist the urge to give her a kiss. Leaning in through the window, he picked her up like a doll and carefully lifted her out into the morning sunlight to give her a giant kiss. The wet sloppiness of Samson's lips gave the woman a very rude awakening. But before Samson could say anything there was a roar of anger, 'What are you doing with my wife?'

It was the young woman's giant husband bringing breakfast for them both.

Panicked, Samson leapt over Holy Austin Rock and stomped off with great strides to make a hasty retreat to his rocky fortress. The young woman began screaming, telling Samson to put her down. Samson was so scared, and then disorientated by the woman's cries, that he ended up heading more towards Compton than to Enville.

The giant husband could not believe what he had seen and started cursing both Samson and his wife. He thought the worst, being under the impression that the two of them had been meeting secretly every morning. He shouted as much over the fields, saying that he wished the two of them dead. In his anger, he searched about for a way to stop the two from escaping and came across a long piece of sandstone, resembling a javelin.

The young woman started shouting now at her husband, telling him that Samson had forced himself on her, that she would never be unfaithful to her love. But her husband was in such a jealous frenzy that he could not hear her words. It was then that the qualities which made her different to other girls came into play. As her husband readied himself to throw the javelin stone at the still escaping Samson, the young woman lifted one hand above her head. She cried out to the sky in a strange high-pitched call, like that of a buzzard but 100 times louder. Then all of a sudden, with not a cloud in the sky, a bolt of lightning hurtled down through the air. It struck Samson, burning him up in a second. At that very moment, the javelin stone came flying through the air and crashed through the sizzling remains of the giant lothario.

The giant husband then rushed over to the stone. His anger seemed to have been spent in that throw of the stony javelin and

now he was in a panic for his wife. She had married him to be her protector and she had been carried away by another giant, only to be struck by lightning. Did anything remain of his beloved?

He could see the javelin stone standing upright from the ground, clearly marking the place where the lightning bolt had struck. And there, tossed to one side of the smoking remains of Samson, lay the giant's wife. She was unharmed, but exhausted. Reaching down, he carefully picked her up in his hands and returned to Kinver. She opened her eyes and smiled weakly.

'I needed to show you I had no feelings for that giant,' she said. 'That is why I called down the lightning.'

'My stone javelin would have finished him off,' her husband replied.

But she closed her eyes and the lost daughter of Thor said no more.

They soon abandoned their home at Holy Austin Rock, but others came later to take up residence there, in that delightful dwelling. The javelin-shaped rock, which stood for many years not far from Compton, became known as the Bolt Stone. Eventually, however, it fell over and sadly, it was broken up and removed. As was the Giant's Water Trough, which had remained at Kinver for many generations. It is a shame that neither of these features remains, but the home at Holy Austin Rock is still there, and it is said to have been immortalised by J.R.R. Tolkien. Those chambers, which operate as liveable houses, have been reported as being the inspiration for Bilbo Baggins' hobbit-hole, Bag End. And so it seems that the giants of Staffordshire are again associated with those of diminutive size.

THE DRAGON OF WEDNESBURY

There was a time when, for many people, the reason for attending church was fear – fear of the Almighty, fear of Hell and fear of what others would say. These all provided a strong motivation to sit in a cold stone building, on a hard wooden pew, to be lectured at, but those who gave regular attendance knew that their ticket to Heaven had been stamped for another week at least. However, the faithful people of Wednesbury soon had a great dilemma; one that was not only as fearsome, but was perhaps more worrying as it was very much a present reality. A dragon had been seen flying over the hills, its great winged shadow hanging over the towns and villages. Many dragons are known for their love of sheep, but this monster had a taste for a different kind of flock. He loved to eat Christians. He felt that they were a healthier alternative, like salad. Perhaps it was knowing that their souls had been washed clean, and that they were sin-free. So, on Sunday mornings he would awake to the pealing of the church bells, which acted as an alarm clock for him. He'd then crawl out of his cave, shake himself out, and open his wings to take to the air. From high up in the clouds, he could see the worshippers of every parish making their way dutifully along well-trodden footpaths, eagerly rushing to their own churches. And he would watch them, carefully deciding which pious congregation to feast on for this particular Sunday. He knew he had a good while to make his decision, as he preferred to wait until they had taken the Eucharist – when they would taste far sweeter.

And so it was that many of the folk of Wednesbury and the surrounding area now went creeping along to church with this new concern. What a quandary they were in. Should they stay at home in case the dragon chose to visit their church? But what would other people say? Some thought that maybe they should trust the Almighty, knowing that he would protect his own if they showed their faith in him by dutiful attendance. Besides, the dragon could very easily visit another church. So, many parishioners would hurry out of their houses, nervously looking to the skies, wondering if they could see the hungry monster, hoping for a clue as to which church was for the eating. However, the dragon was hidden high up in the fluffy clouds and was not so easily seen from the ground.

Across the region, quaking congregations would gather behind bolted church doors to sing hymns (not too loudly), say the liturgy (in a whisper) and pray that the vicar would not preach for long. And when it finally came to the Eucharist, many would take the wafer and wine in relief, thinking that there was not much more of the service to go and they had been spared. When suddenly the dragon would crash through the great stained-glass window above the altar. Leaping into the chancel he would gobble up the priest and then chase the screaming congregation through the nave, with many of them tripping over the pews. Rarely would any escape because those carefully bolted church doors would trap them and the dragon would invariably enjoy a great Sunday feast; healthy, wholesome and holy. Whole congregations were to him a delicious dish of salmagundi.

After a while, church attendances were noticeably waning. Not only because, increasingly, people were choosing not to come, but also because each week there was one less church in the area with a living congregation. So the dragon turned his eye to the townsfolk. Occasionally, on some of his weekday flights, he had seen the stately procession of the town council in their robes and chains of office. They were an attractive bunch, but he had also seen the size of some of them. If truth be told, the dragon was beginning to get a bit bored with healthy eating and fancied something a little more flavoursome. He felt he deserved a little treat.

He gave the churches a miss that Sunday and hopped over onto the roof of the town hall. As Monday morning came and the council, led by the fat jolly mayor with his mace of office, came marching through the town, the dragon licked his lips. He waited until they were all seated and all the pomp and ceremony was over. Then he crashed through the ceiling, throwing the council into a mad panic. They ran about the chambers screaming and tripping over their robes, but they didn't rush about with as much speed as the parishioners. They were, in fact, very easy to catch and one by one the dragon flipped them into his wide open jaws, enjoying a hearty, tasty meal. Then the beast noticed that the mayor was still sitting in his chair. He was asleep – somehow snoozing through the dragon-spawned anarchy. Oh, this was too easy and what a sumptuous dish to finish off such a feast. But then, the dragon wasn't so sure that he should eat a further morsel at that point. He did feel a bit bloated and thought that he mustn't be too greedy. He slid over to the sleeping official. 'Hmm,' he thought, 'this was the mayor.' With all the pies and wine that he consumed, he was certainly going to taste good, a full rich delicacy no doubt. And so, against his better judgement, he lifted the chair and tipped the mayor into his mouth. The man never knew what had happened, and may have been the better for it.

Then, knowing he was just a little too full, the dragon sidled out of the double doors of those chambers and onto the steps of the town hall, where he picked his teeth with the mace of office.

'Ooh,' he thought. The dragon didn't feel good. His eyes had been bigger than his stomach and now he was regretting it. There was a peculiar gurgling from within and if he had not been a dragon you would say that he had gone an odd shade of green. But he was green to begin with, and so nobody knew the difference. He knew it though and began to panic. He looked about anxiously. Where could he be sick? But he didn't have time to worry more about it. A great, fiery belch came thundering up from his stomach, into his throat and then … the dragon exploded. The half-chewed remains of the town council, mayor and all, were splattered all over the street. Slimy chunks stuck onto shop windows and signposts and an acrid, stinking vomit dripped from the church spire. As for the dragon, the people of Wednesbury discovered bits and pieces of his remains in the most obscure places for many years thereafter. And whenever they found a remnant of that greedy beast, they would nod sagely and say, 'Ah, that's what

comes of swallowing whole the offerings of the mayor and his town council.'

The Dragon of Wednesbury churches ate –

(He used to come on Sunday) –

Whole congregations were to him

A dish of salmagundi.

The corporation worshipful

He valued not an ace

But swallowed the mayor, asleep in his chair,

And picked his teeth with a mace.

BIBLIOGRAPHY

Baker, M., *Folklore & Customs of Rural England* (David & Charles, 1974)

Burnim, K.A., Highfill, P.H. & Langhans, E.A., *A Biographical Dictionary of Actors: Vol. I* (Southern Illinois University Press, 1973)

Coleman, S.J., *Staffordshire Folklore* (Unpublished, 1955)

Gibson, A., *Staffordshire Legends* (Churnet Valley Books, 2002)

Greenslade, M., *Catholic Staffordshire* (Gracewing, 2006)

Hackwood, F.W., *Staffordshire Customs, Superstitions and Folklore* (Mercury Press, 1924)

Hollins, T.J., *Weird Tales of Staffordshire* (Debony, 2000)

Kent, J., *The Mysterious Double Sunset* (Witan Books, 2001)

Lawrence-Smith, K., *Tales of Old Staffordshire* (Countryside Books, 1992)

Leigh, F., *North Staffordshire: Myths and Legends* (Staffs Publishing, 2011)

Long, G., *Penny Cyclopedia of the Society for the Diffusion of Useful Knowledge: Vol. XIII* (Society for the Diffusion of Useful Knowledge, 1839)

Mee, A., *Staffordshire: Beauty and the Black Country* (King's England series) (Caxton, 1937)

Pickford, D., *Myths and Legends of East Cheshire and the Moorlands* (Sigma Leisure, 1992)

Pickford, D., *Staffordshire: Its Magic and Mystery* (Sigma Leisure, 1994)

Poulton-Smith, A., *Staffordshire Place Names* (Countryside Books, 1995)

Raven, J., *The Folklore of Staffordshire* (Batsford Ltd, 1978)

Wedgwood, H.A., *People of the Potteries* (Adams & Dart, 1970)

If you enjoyed this book, you may also be interested in…

Cheshire Folk Tales

THE JOURNEY MAN

These lively and entertaining folk tales from one of Britain's most ancient counties are vividly retold by local storyteller The Journey Man. Their origins lost in the oral tradition, these thirty stories from Cheshire reflect the wisdom (and eccentricities) of the county and its people. These stories, illustrated with twenty-five line drawings, bring alive the landscape of the county's rolling hills and fertile plains.

978 0 7524 6513 5

Haunted Staffordshire

PHILIP SOLOMON

From heart-stopping accounts of apparitions, manifestations and related supernatural phenomena to first-hand encounters with ghouls and spirits, this collection of stories contains both new and well-known spooky stories from around Staffordshire. It is compiled by the Wolverhampton Express & Star's own psychic agony uncle, Philip Solomon. Haunted Staffordshire is sure to fascinate everyone with an interest in the area's haunted history.

978 0 7524 6168 7

Gloucestershire Folk Tales

ANTHONY NANSON

Gloucestershire's layers of story go back to the days of Sabrina, spirit of the Severn, and the Nine Hags of Gloucester. This collection of tales includes sky-ships over Bristol, the silk-caped wraith of Dover's Hill, and the snow foresters on the Cotswolds. From the intrigue and romance of town and abbey to the fairy magic of the wild, here are thirty of the county's most enchanting tales, brought imaginatively to life by a dynamic local storyteller.

978 0 7524 6017 8

Visit our website and discover thousands of other History Press books.

www.thehistorypress.co.uk